Praise for *Between Methods & Madness*

"Erik's premise is very thought-provoking! Erik is tenacious in getting every little detail correct. This book is extremely well-researched and makes you feel like you are present in London and Normandy in June 1944!"

—**Paul McLaughlin**, US Army Captain, Rangers Lead the Way

"In *Between Methods & Madness,* Dr. Erik Függer is pulled back to 1944 to prevent the Nazis from sabotaging the Normandy invasion. After a car accident leaves him questioning reality, Erik must unravel the mystery behind a failed D-Day and restore the timeline before history is forever changed. Erik Foge masterfully blends suspense and historical fiction in this thrilling read.

—**Bob Babcock**, 4th Infantry Division Association Historian

BETWEEN
METHODS & MADNESS

BETWEEN
METHODS & MADNESS
ERIK FOGE

Deeds Publishing | Athens

Published by Deeds Publishing in Athens, GA
www.deedspublishing.com

Printed in The United States of America

Cover design by Mark Babcock.

ISBN 978-1-961505-29-2

Books are available in quantity for promotional or premium use. For information, email info@deedspublishing.com.

First Edition, 2024

10 9 8 7 6 5 4 3 2 1

This book is dedicated to my amazing, loving, and supportive wife, Kristina, and all my fans who made the journey with Dr. Erik Függer throughout the *Project Pegasus* series.

"Everything I write has a precedent in truth."   —Ian Fleming

VANISHING INTO SOUNDS OF SILENCE

"Torment, for some men, is a need, an appetite, and an accomplishment."

—Emile M. Cioran

Dripping blood, enough to form puddles, echoed in a poorly lit room. The crimson fluid flowed like rivers down the body of a man strapped to a chair, his flesh cut by rope fibers. A stately, handsome man in a crisp, black SS Colonel uniform hovered over the man, sighed inwardly, and looked toward the man's battered and bruised face, its eyelids darkened shades of blue, purple, and black. The colonel gently prodded the man. "We still need to talk."

The man shook his head.

"Let me introduce myself. I am Colonel Apophis Adelram," he said in a warm, caring voice as he wrung out a damp washcloth with a powerful grip. Long, narrow fingers were attached to his large hands. He wiped blood from the man's forehead as he looked down at him. "I am unlike the other ruthless SS men you have met." He paused as if he were relishing the moment.

"Major Schan, I have some good news." He emphasized his next words. "I am a medical doctor who can help you with your pain."

The major's eyes darted to several vials of morphine in plain view on a nearby table. The colonel smiled. "I see you noticed the morphine on the table. I can assure you I am a man of my word. Give me what I need, and the pain will stop."

Apophis strode around the table, which was also stacked with an intimidating array of neatly arranged manila folders. He grabbed a newspaper and strolled toward the major. "Major Schan, as you can see, we know all about your invasion." He lifted the newspaper, carefully unfolded it, and glanced over it with cold, calculating blue eyes. "I know you've heard of the New York Times…"

Major Schan nodded subtly.

"If you don't believe me, read it yourself."

Major Schan struggled to open his eyes. The headline read: *ALLIED ARMIES FAIL TO LAND IN FRANCE ON THE NORMANDY COAST; GREAT LOSS OF LIFE; EISENHOWER STEPS DOWN.* Silence filled the room other than the major's shallow breaths and the humming of the lights in the room. Schan slowly craned his neck to stare back at Apophis. The major tried to murmur something, but his body language, amid all the bruises and blood, was what Apophis needed.

Apophis stepped back to the table and lifted a syringe and a cotton ball with rubbing alcohol on it. "Major Schan, I forgot to keep my word." Apophis's eyes shone every facet of evil one might imagine. They reflected immense cruelty and brutality, an absence of remorse, ambition, and willingness to sacrifice everything for his goals and the survival of the Nazi party and the Reich. Apophis lacked regard for human life, remorse, and empathy, which made him successful at what he did. He injected twenty ccs of air into the major's vein. He observed the major's body, watching dispassionately as the man gasped and spasmed, struggling to draw breath as his lungs failed him, and finally mewled a whimper filled with pain before going limp. Standing quiet for several minutes, he admired his work, staring at the lifeless corpse of the military intelligence officer. His mission complete, his eyes blazed with excitement.

Apophis walked out with the fake New York Times, strolled up the stairs, and down the main corridor, where the top brass waited for a report. It was nearing 0600 hours. He approached a set of double doors that were guarded by sentries. They snapped to attention and swung the entrance open. He strode into a vast room, surrounded by individuals carrying folders and opening and closing filing cabinet doors. In an adjoining room, operators answered muted telephones. In another, people crossed with Teletype strips bearing weather reports and updates on troop movements. Several individuals, a part of the German High Command of Western Europe, analyzed a long table with a map of southern England, northern France, and the low countries marked with the positions of their units and the Allies' units. Apophis approached the table and caught the end of the Luftwaffe's chief meteorologist, Colonel Professor Walter Stobe's, briefing.

Rundstedt and Rommel looked on, their silence inviting further explanation.

"I'm predicting increasing cloudiness, high winds, and rain."

Rundstedt dismissed Stobe, stared at Apophis, and said in a high, authoritative, and impatient tone. "What did you find out, Herr Colonel?"

Apophis walked forward with purpose, holding eye contact with the field marshals. He tossed the fake newspaper on the map and replied. "I got what we needed."

"I disapprove of your methods," Rundstedt said bitterly.

"You may dislike how I obtain information, but I always get results." He pointed to the newspaper headline about a failed landing in Normandy. "I will call Hitler's adjutant, Major General

Rudolf Schmundt, to advise the Führer." Then, in a calm yet demanding tone, Apophis ordered, "Alert the 68th Corps, under General der Infanterie Sponheimer, and have him move the 64th Static Infantry Division, 346th Infantry Division, and the 711th Static Division of the Seventh Army from Pas de Calais to Normandy now." Then he faced Rommel and ordered him, with no interference from Von Rundstedt, to have the 21st and the 12th SS Panzer Divisions move to the coast of Normandy.

Stepping back from the map table, Apophis proclaimed, "We are now prepared for the allied landings. This will all happen in thirty-six hours."

CHAPTER 1

LOVERS AND THEN THE LONER

"To be half of one can only be a torment when the other half is gone."   —Richard Matheson, *What Dreams May Come*

KENNEDY WARREN, WASHINGTON D.C., JANUARY 18, 1960

Jamie hovered over the stove, noise from utensils echoing in the kitchen as she prepares breakfast and aromas filling the kitchen and dining room. Max, age fifteen, and D'Artagnan, age eleven, tucked their homework and books into their backpacks as they wait patiently for their food. Erik pulled out their lunches and placed them in front of each boy as he took his seat.

"Mom, can you make pancakes sometime?" Max hoped his mom would recognize his request.

Adding the final touches to the eggs and bacon, Jamie looked over her shoulder with a warm smile and shook her head. "I have told you guys before that if you want pancakes, you need to get up earlier."

"I can get something at school." Erik tilted his head and narrowed his eyes at Max, which stopped his pleading.

"You've got to eat something now." She served everyone in equal portions.

"Hey, you know what?" Max blurted out between mouthfuls. "This Friday, our history class is having some dads come in and talk about what they did in World War Two."

Jamie shot a subtle glance at Erik.

"Can you come to talk to my class, Dad?"

Erik shook his head.

Max frowned, "Why not?"

"Because I cannot talk about what I did," Erik said as he motioned for him to finish breakfast. In addition, Erik didn't have to explain himself to adults because they accepted things at face value. However, with his kids, that was a different story. They thought it was cool to brag to their friends. Eventually, they would understand why he couldn't talk about the war.

Jamie stepped in to help. "Max, all you need to know is your father worked for the government." She tilted her head as she folded her arms against her chest.

"Dad," Max continued as Erik peered over his papers. "Were you in the European or Pacific Theater?"

Erik placed his papers down.

"I hear from other boys what their fathers did, but I don't know what you did."

Erik gestured to Jamie that it was okay as he addressed Max firmly. "It's like when we do war gaming," he explained in basic terms. "I had to be five steps ahead of our enemies, find a solution, and resolve any problems."

It baffled Max as Erik continued, "All I can tell you is that the people I worked for were never ashamed of my abilities." Max nodded again. "I know you don't understand, but believe me, I served my country just as much as those who wore the uniform. Understood?"

"Thanks, Dad," Max replied as Erik motioned him to finish his breakfast.

Jamie's attention shifted when D'Artagnan barged in. "Mom, can you pick me up early tomorrow?"

Jamie looked at him for an explanation.

He rolled his eyes. "Because I won't have to wait after school and listen to some boring guy talk about art history. I would rather learn about drawing from you."

"Sorry, your father and I have a meeting. We're planning to pick you up after we get your brother," Jamie explained. She then added, turning the negative into a positive, "Then, we'll all go out for pizza." Smiles filled the room. She knelt and looked lovingly at D'Artagnan. "We'll see your artwork in the school's gallery tomorrow."

"I thought you guys couldn't make it."

"We don't want to miss it." Jamie looked at Erik for confirmation.

He grinned and nodded at D'Artagnan.

"We're late, guys!" Jamie declared after glancing at her watch, then grabbed her purse and car keys.

"Hey, Max, keep a buttoned lip about me and the war, okay?"

"Yeah," Max smiled and wished to be like his father and work for the government. "Love you, Dad," he added as he headed to the door. He turned around one last time. "Dad, can we do some war gaming after I do my homework?"

Erik nodded and followed behind his family.

D'Artagnan hugged Erik and whispered. "I hate listening to art history. I prefer drawing."

"Me too."

Jerry Greene, the doorman at the Kennedy Warren, greeted Erik, Jamie, and the boys as they raced to the car and Jamie made her way to the driver's side. She motioned to Erik and said she would be back in one hour.

Erik leaned over to the passenger window and addressed each of the boys. "Max, don't always correct Mr. Hardle in history class."

Max nodded.

"D'Artagnan, your mother puts healthy stuff in your lunchbox for you to eat for lunch." D'Artagnan and Erik continued in unison, in near complete harmony, "Don't trade it for chips and cookies."

Erik waved goodbye as the car disappeared down the road. It was the last time he saw them alive.

CHAPTER 2

FROM THE DARKNESS COMES KNOWLEDGE AND DOUBT

"The intellectual side of man already admits that life is an incessant struggle for existence."

—H. G. Wells, *The War of the Worlds*

THE WHITE HOUSE, CABINET ROOM, WASHINGTON D.C., MAY 26, 1961

The confident and powerful President Kennedy strode down the hallway. Bobby Kennedy, Attorney General of the United States, and Kenny O'Donnell, Special Assistant to the President, walked on either side of him to the Cabinet Room. Prior to then, they were discussing Fulgencio Batista y Zaldívar.

In 1940, he was elected president of Cuba for the first time after a distinguished career as a military officer. Several times before 1944, Hitler and Zaldívar met each other to discuss possible alliances. Cuba became a satellite country of the Third Reich in the year following the unsuccessful invasion of Normandy. Fidel Castro, a US-backed revolutionary military leader, led a brief but devastating coup in Cuba between July 26, 1953 and January 1, 1959, later known as the Cuban Revolution, against Zaldívar's government. The Cuban president reached out to Hitler, who generously provided him with weapons and equipment.

Following the victory over the revolution, Zaldívar made it possible for Hitler to establish military bases in Cuba. From there, the Führer drew up plans to attack American cities through the use of land and submarine launched rockets. Furthermore, a number of Luftwaffe airstrips and a U-boat base were built in order to sink American ships. Last, but not least, Hitler was also building an amphibious fleet intending to attack the USA in a plan known as Operation Eberhard Mantey.

By the time President Kennedy and his entourage were within six feet of the Cabinet Room, Secret Service agents threw open the massive double doors. Around the table were the hard-ass men of the United States Executive Committee of the National Security Council (EXCOM), who advise the president. The president, known to many as Jack, exchanged small talk with the dozen assembled officials as he made his way to his chair. The dozen men, all clean cut in their youthful forties to mid-fifties and wearing designer blue or gray suits, gathered around an ornate, Roosevelt-era table and focused their attention on Jack.

In unison, the men in the room said, "Good morning, Mr. President."

"Good morning, gentlemen."

Everyone followed the president's lead and took their seats as soon as he did so. At the head of the table. Dean Rusk, the Secretary of State, and Avery Herrera, the Secretary of the Department of War, sat on either side of the president. Bobby took an overstuffed chair at the table and Kenny found a chair behind the President, under the window to the Rose Garden, next to Ted Sorensen, the President's legal counsel. The president's speechwriter sat next to him. There was a moment of silence throughout the room as President Kennedy looked across the table toward

General Marshall Carter, Deputy Chief of Operations for the Central Intelligence Agency. "Okay, General, what do we know of now?" Jack asked.

At that point, Carter introduced Arthur Lundahl, who was a member of the photographic interpretation division of the CIA. During his remarks, he informed everyone that Lundahl would be running through what data they had as of 0800 hours on Tuesday morning. After a moment of pause, Carter looked at Lundahl and gave him a nod to begin his briefing.

Lundahl stood by a briefing board covered in a large map of the Caribbean and several aerial spy plane photographs with a pointer in his hand to aid him with his presentation. He looked around the room, then focused on the president. "Gentlemen, one of our U-2s flew over Cuba on Tuesday morning and took a series of troubling photographs."

He stepped sideways and used the pointer to emphasize several key points. "We know the Nazis are continuing to build launch sites in Los Palacios, Cuba, for their EMW A8 rockets, also known as the Super V-2. They can deliver a one-megaton nuclear weapon one thousand nautical miles."

He paused for a moment. "We do not believe these missiles are operational yet." He once again looked around the room, then proclaimed, "So far, we have identified twenty missiles served by around two thousand men, undoubtedly all Nazi personnel." He then touched several places on the map. "We also discovered the Luftwaffe has several Me1108/1 long-range bombers that can carry a payload of twenty-two hundred pounds of bombs with the range of one thousand and eighty nautical miles."

He dragged the pointer along the northern coast of Cuba. "Our analysis shows that the Nazis have followed their conventional weapons build-up with tanks, personnel, and landing crafts."

"So, if I understand you correctly," Jack rubbed his chin as he studied the map, "our cities and military installations in the Southeast, and as far north as Washington DC, are in a range of these weapons."

"That's correct, Mr. President."

"In the event of a launch, how much of a warning would we have?"

"Mr. President, we would only have ten minutes of warning."

General Carter cut in, "Ten minutes, gentlemen."

General Taylor added to the conversation, "In those ten minutes, they could do significant damage."

Jack looked at him with an unspoken invitation to explain further.

"Ninety-five million Americans would be killed," General Taylor explained, "and they could destroy a substantial number of our B-52 bomber bases." He took a deep breath. "If that happens, they could launch an amphibious landing in Florida. Mr. President, that would degrade our retaliatory options."

Jack remained calm as the general continued. "Mr. President, the Joint Chiefs' consensus is that this is a massively destabilizing move. Australia and The United States are the only two major powers fighting the Nazis. Because they're barely hanging on, we can't count on the Soviet Union."

Each man in the room grappled with their own fears but hid them.

Bobby cut in, "General, how long until the missiles are operational?"

General Taylor did a quick calculation in his head, then replied, "GMAIC estimates nine to eleven days. However, if they rush, they could cut that time." Grim looks filled the room as he continued. "I have to stress that there may be more missiles that we don't know about." He stared at the president. "Sir, we need more U-2 coverage to determine that."

The president nodded and leaned forward. "Is there any indication the Nazis intend to use these missiles in some sort of pre-invasion strike?"

General Carter let out a deep sigh, "Sir, since we have refused to sign a peace treaty with Hitler, I think there is no doubt the Nazis will attack and they will do so with everything they have. The question is: When?"

The president asked, "Do we have any sort of intelligence from the CIA on that?"

General Carter shook his head. "No, Mr. President, we don't. We just don't know what's happening inside the inner circle of Hitler's headquarters."

The President nodded and said without hesitation, "Gentlemen, I want first reactions. Assuming for a moment Hitler intends to attack us, what are we looking at?"

At the end of the table was Rusk's team: George Ball, Alexis Johnson, Edwin Martin, Llewellyn Thompson, and Adlai Stevenson. Rusk used nonverbal communication, which only he and his team understood. Then, he turned to face the president and said with the utmost confidence, "Mr. President, I believe my team is in agreement. If we permit an attack by the Nazis in our hemisphere, especially on the United States, the diplomatic and military consequences will be too terrible to contemplate."

He looked around the room. "The Nazis are trying to show the world they can do whatever they want, wherever they want, and we're powerless to stop them."

Bobby voiced his opinion, "It will be like the invasion of Poland all over again, and it will leave Australia to fend for themselves."

Rusk added, "If we surrender to the Nazis, the world will falter." He nodded in Bobby's direction, "Australia will become unsure in the face of Nazi pressure, which will embolden the Reich to advance even further. We must stop them."

He tapped the table with his index finger to stress his next point. "It seems to me we have two options. One, let them build up their arsenal unchecked 'til they attack, or two, we hit them with an air strike and our nuclear arsenal before they can make a move."

Dead silence engulfed the room, with some nods of understanding.

The president turned to Herrera for his advice. "Avery?"

"We've worked up several military scenarios." He glanced at General Taylor and then back at the president. "Before I ask General Taylor to lead us through the various options, I'd like for us to adopt a rule. If we are intending to strike, we must agree now that we will do it before the missiles become operational and that we will destroy their bombers and their landing craft. If we wait, we can't guarantee to get all their missiles before at least some are launched. Also, we must stop their armada from reaching the Florida coast. Mr. President, the clock is running."

McGeorge Bundy, the National Security Advisor, warned with a sense of calm that was becoming rare in the room, "Mr. President, we need to consider that if we decide to attack, there's a high chance we'll end up fighting the Nazis for years. Moreover, they are stronger. We might not win."

Again, the room fell silent.

The president leaned back in his chair, studying the circle of men around the table, weighing their opinions. Silence hung in the room, as everyone was either scared to add more tension or simply terrified into silence by the threat of the war coming to their doorsteps.

Finally, Bundy continued, "No matter what happens from this point forward, it will change the course of history, and any decision we make here today will decide how."

The President leaned forward, folded his hands on the table, and looked around the room. "It's clear we cannot permit the Nazis to place nuclear missiles in Cuba or have them attack us on the Florida coast. We must stop them, no matter the cost."

CHAPTER 3

THE DAY LOST IN TIME

"Evil brings men together."

—Aristotle

THE WHITE HOUSE, WASHINGTON D.C.

The president stood as the meeting adjourned, and everyone rose, knowing what needed done before the next time they met. Jack returned to the Oval Office with Kenny and Bobby following. Each composed their body language as the morning's shock wore off. Jack stopped, looked at them, and whispered, "I don't think it's going to matter what Hitler's intentions are." He leaned forward so only they could hear him. "I tell you; I don't see any way around hitting them. The Nazis have made their intention and objective clear."

"Either way, if they strike first or if we do, the war is coming home," Kenny declared. For the first time, the faces of all three men felt the true enormity of the threat.

Bobby added, "Even if we stop them, we'll be at war with the Nazis somewhere else in six months."

The president turned away and continued down the hall, the others following as he contemplated their options and the potential consequences of the decision looming over them. They stepped into the reception area helmed by Evelyn Lincoln, President Kennedy's personal secretary, and Jack said, "There are no alternatives. We have to strike first and bomb them."

"General Taylor says we may have some time before they can arm their missiles," Bobby stated. "We've got to use that time to our advantage."

"So, if there are no alternatives that make sense, that sounds like our only option. They'll still invade, but it will be easier to defend ourselves against their amphibious assault if we strike first."

"What about the allies?" Bobby asked.

"Australia?" Kenny derided as he shook his head. "It's unlikely they will be able to help. They have their own issues, and the Russians are barely defending themselves against the Nazis. They have been fighting since 1941."

***

Immediately after the failure of the D Day invasion on 6 June 1944, the Germans learned about Operation Anvil (better known as Operation Dragoon), a plan for the allied invasion of southern France. German forces were composed of Army Group G, poorly equipped troops, with the 11th Panzer Division being the only formidable unit. However, the one advantage the Germans had was seventy five coastal gun placements amounting to 1,481 artillery pieces. The Germans knew the Allies still had air superiority, so moving troops from northern to southern France would not be effective as they would simply bomb the coastal defenses at Toulon and west of Cannes.

Not only that, they knew the French resistance would sabotage fortifications, railroads, and anything of strategic importance. Because of that, the Germans placed elaborate piping around certain locations to release Sarin, an extreme potency as a nerve agent, along the coast. Despite low concentrations in such a widespread release, exposure to the substance was normally fatal. Unless antidotes are administered within one minute of direct inhalation of a lethal dose, a person might suffocate and die within ten minutes due to respiratory paralysis. In those cases, because of the unimaginable hell the chemicals put the body through, the lucky ones die fast.

On August 15, 1944, Operation Dragoon began with successful Allied landings and the paratrooper drops at Le Muy known as Codename Rugby. This played into the German's plan, as their troops were given gas masks, and the Allied soldiers were not. The unprepared Allied troops were devastated once the Sarin was released, and their advance came to a halt. Meanwhile, at Le Muy, the Germans were prepared for the French Resistance and the paratroopers, both of whom were met with more Sarin and better prepared troops.

Once Churchill learned about this, he strongly urged the military and his cabinet to go along with his plan known as Operation Vegetarian. Churchill, who in March of 1944 ordered five hundred thousand anthrax bombs from America, was planning to use them on six German cities, thus infecting the German food supply. However, this was met with resistance and several advised Churchill the Germans would retaliate with something worse. So, the British and Americans amplified their heavy bombing campaigns on civilian, military, and industrial targets.

After the failure of Operation Dragoon, Germany Nazified the Free French territories in France and Africa, increasing their military by one point three million men by September of 1944. Germany was then able to force Portugal to capitulate. The country, ruled by António de Oliveira Salazar—who founded the Estado Novo corporatist authoritarian government—effectively became a client state of the Third Reich.

Spain, under Francisco Franco, espoused neutrality as its official wartime policy, which gave way to non-belligerence after the Fall of France in June 1940. However, Hitler threatened to enact Operation Felix, the proposed German invasion of Spain and seizure of Gibraltar, if Franco wouldn't make Spain a vassal state of Germany or give up his sovereignty. Again, Franco told Hitler that Spain would continue to espouse neutrality.

Hitler promised Salazar of Portugal territory in Spain if he assisted with the invasion of Spain. On October 31, 1944, Spain was attacked from southern France and on its western border from Portugal. Franco was caught off guard, and by mid-November, he fled the country. Spain surrendered, and Germany seized control of the skies over Europe. Before the formal surrender, German attacked Gibraltar to seize the ships of the Royal Navy by an air-supported ground assault of four conventional infantry regiments, one paratrooper regiment, three engineer battalions, and twelve artillery regiments. The Kriegsmarine used their E-boats, who had infantry on board with the crew, to board the ships of the Royal Navy, and the E-boats prevented the ships from escaping.

While all that was happening, the Germans pushed the British out of North Africa, and seized the Suez Canal, reconquered the Italian peninsula, and secured the battle line with the USSR.

Reich Minister of Armaments and War Production Albert Speer and Admiral Karl Dönitz convinced Hitler to focus on rebuilding the U-boat fleet with the new Type XXI. Between 1943 and December 1944, sixty boats were assembled and completed by Blohm & Voss of Hamburg, AG Weser of Bremen, and Schichau-Werke of Danzig. The new Type XXI U-boats, equipped with acoustic-homing torpedoes and a revolutionary fire control system, were positioned around England and in the Atlantic. In time, they began to carry out effective attacks, even when totally submerged. In addition, with a radar absorbent material coating the hull, they were undetectable to surface vessels at a mere 220 yards away. After striking, the XXI could escape at maximum speed, fifteen knots, at which speed the allies' sonar was totally ineffective. In only a few months, the XXI affected allied shipping, including warships.

In addition, Speer, with help from Hans Kammler — responsible for the V-2 rocket-program — sped production on the rockets and established launch sites in France. Speer stressed the targets should be the bomber airfields and coastal defenses.

By December 1944, the Germans had regained control of the Atlantic and started gaining air superiority over Europe because of their jets and V2 strikes on Allied air bases. American forces started to leave England, and the Royal Navy attempted to evacuate Canada with disastrous results, as more squadrons of U-Boats were waiting for them in the North Atlantic.

From there, Turkey and several African nations started negotiations to become satellites of the Third Reich. Both Germany and the USSR quickly make alliances or conquered countries in the Middle East to control the oil fields. Germany had control of Saudi Arabia and Iraq, while the USSR had Iran. Once Africa and the Middle East were stabilized, Germany focused on South America and the Caribbean. By 1959, Germany had control of most of the world. It was only a matter of time until Germany launched their next attack.

The US Presidential election in 1944 was difficult for Roosevelt and Truman. Unlike in 1940, Roosevelt faced little opposition within his own party, even though there were major setbacks in the land war in Europe.

After the failures of Operations Overlord and Dragoon, there was a growing pacifist movement in America. Thomas E. Dewey, the Republican nominee, aligned with this and advocated for an immediate withdrawal of the United States from Europe.

In addition, Americans were discouraged by bomber crew losses and believed daylight bombings were a mistake and should be discontinued. Thus, the majority of people believed that the United States should enter into bilateral peace negotiations with Germany. Because of this, the Reich had time to complete its heavy-water experiments and develop the atomic bomb before the Americans.

Hitler threatened to use atomic-armed V2 rockets on any nation who opposed the Reich, ensuring there would be little or no resistance to Germany's global conquest. Churchill, King George VI and his wife, and members of the Houses of Commons and Lords fled for Canada. To prevent England from being devastated, on December 10, 1945, Edward VIII sat on the English throne with Wallis Simpson by his side.

Dewey was right about making a separate peace with Germany, but it was the wrong time. Roosevelt easily won the presidential nomination of the 1944 Democratic National Convention since there was no other candidate available, and Senator Harry S. Truman was chosen to be Roosevelt's vice president. Both Roosevelt and Truman campaigned on the United States staying in the war, saying Germany would eventually bring the conflict to America's front door if they weren't stopped overseas.

Dewey on the eve of the 1944 election, delivered a passionate speech: *"We stand today on one of the strange promontories of human history, with the shadows of a dismal stormy night behind us, and the first gray streaks of dawn in the sky beyond us. For thirty years since 1914, nearly half the span of human life, we have seen a series of wars, revolutions, depressions, communism, fascism, Nazism, cruelty and suffering, and finally, another conflagration that has engulfed the world. At home, we have had twelve unhappy years of turmoil and dissension, of group conflict and class strife, of divisions, and hatreds, and antagonisms. Half a generation has grown up knowing no other atmosphere. I believe our children, our whole country, can again live in a world where peace, friendship, and mutual respect abide."*[1]

This resonated with most Americans, and on November 7, 1944, Dewey became the thirty-third President of the United States.

***

Bobby glanced at Kenny and Jack. "I think we may need to let key people know, including Congress."

The President said, "We can't worry about everything right now. We've got to figure out when we're going to attack, and how, before we have anything substantive to tell Congress."

"The Joint Chiefs are going to be pressing for a military attack soon," Bobby said.

Kenny started, "The other thing is—"

"The other thing is," a new voice interjected, "that there is another way we can defeat and contain the Nazis."

All three men looked at the newcomer and his entourage, whom Evelyn introduced. "Mr. President, these men are from an intelligence group known as ONE and would like to speak to you."

Jack gave a subtle nod to Kenny, who approached the men. "Defeat and contain the Nazis? Gentlemen, the president has a lot of work to do. I'm asking you to leave." Kenny snapped his fingers at a pair of nearby Secret Service Agents, signaling them to remove the uninvited guests. "I'll see they escort you gentlemen from the White House."

"Before you kick us out, let me introduce myself. I'm George H. Scherff. I was Nikola Tesla's assistant, and currently work on

---

1. Source: https://www.youtube.com/watch?v=aBqYsDrDmd...

Project Pegasus, which is a time-travel exploration program." He handed Kenny several front pages from The New York Times.

Kenny, Bobby, and Jack thumbed through the pages, growing more astonished with each one.

Scherff continued, "I'm showing you events that will happen. The question is, are you willing to change them?"

"The way this administration is intending to change it is we are going to bomb the hell out of the Nazis in Cuba, not by entertaining delusions about time travel and looking at fake newspapers, goddamnit!" Kenny exclaimed.

"If you do that, before you can celebrate, the Nazis will launch their A10 rockets, each with a ten-megaton nuclear warhead," Szigeti pointed at Kennedy. "This is a war you cannot win. The results will change history and end this country. When the dust settles, the Nazis will rule over the ashes of what used to be the United States of America."

"You said we can defeat and contain the Nazis?" Jack asked, his eyes still scanning the newspapers.

Scherff nodded, "To do that, we need to look at June 6, 1944."

"Mr. President, this is ridiculous," Kenny barked. "Project Pegasus? Time Travel? These men are wasting time we can't afford." He then grabbed and tossed the newspapers in the trash.

"The Nazis will respond with nuclear weapons," Scherff warned.

"Jesus Christ, are you psychic now? You are worse than the CIA. They and the military fucked us on the Bay of Pigs." Kenny made a crude hand gesture to illustrate his point. He laughed, shook his head, and pointed at the crumpled up newspapers in the trash bin. "Every novelty shop can print a phony newspaper. If you're going to make absurd claims about time travel to the president, you better come up with something more concrete than this garbage."

"I know of an event that happened in August 1943 in the Solomon Islands. A sniper was supposed to kill a young naval lieutenant who is now President of the United States."

Both Kenny and Bobby look at Jack, dumbfounded. Jack turned to Evelyn. "Call Erik at his house. Tell him I need him here now. If you can't get him, send Secret Service agents out to find him. He could be at the Old City Cemetery in Lynchburg, Virginia if he is not at home. Either way, find him and bring him to me."

CHAPTER 4

THE FRONT PORCH OF HEAVEN

"They were there when you had something to tell. They were there when you walked through life. Don't worry, you will see them soon… but not yet."

—Erik Foge

KENNEDY WARREN, WASHINGTON D.C., MAY 26, 1961

Erik's eyes snapped open to a dark room. His face was alert, tense, and bathed in sweat, as if he were having a nightmare or an unpleasant dream. Another tiring, restless night. He took a deep sigh as he looked at her pillow, having hoped she would be there. He rolled over to the edge of the bed and turned on the lamp. His eyes moistened as loneliness filled him up inside as he stared at the pictures of Jamie in her wedding dress and their two sons.

Sitting upright in the bed, Erik wiped the tears from his eyes while pulling out the Luger from under his pillow. He started breathing hard, adrenalin pumping through his veins as he stared at the pistol with his finger on the trigger. He wanted to end his pain, and his entire body quaked with rage. Erik turned the barrel to touch his forehead as his finger squeezed back on the trigger, yet he couldn't do it. He threw the Luger across the room while tears ran down his face. He had been living without Jamie's love for nearly sixteen months since she and the boys died in the car accident.

After he composed himself, Erik finally got up, did his morning rituals, got dressed, and headed out the door.

OLD CITY CEMETERY, LYNCHBURG, VIRGINIA

In the rear of the cemetery, away from monuments in the Confederate section and other burial sites, Erik walked under the towering oak trees whose branching canopy provided shade below. Beautiful gardens filled with hundreds of varieties of native and heirloom plants surrounded him. He was alone across the cemetery. As ice rain drizzled, pools formed in several areas between the gravestones, running through channels carved over the years. Two groundskeepers stood and watched him, as they did every Saturday morning. Rain, snow, holidays—nothing kept him away. Erik stood over the three two-foot by one-foot, polished, black marble grave markers.

JAMIE LYNN FOGE 1921 - 1960
MAX VON FOGE 1945 – 1960
D'ARTAGNAN FOGE 1949 – 1960

He knelt down and brushed leaves from the grave markers. Wistfully, he forced a sorrowful smile at their names as he fought back tears, lamenting how their lives were cut short. He looked up at the gray clouds rolling in from the Atlantic, his expression changing into a tense rage, as he uttered, "You didn't need to take them."

A crack of thunder pierced Erik's ears as the drizzle transformed into steady rain and a chill consumed the graveyard. The rain hid his tears as he wiped them away. He slumped his head and fought to keep his voice level as he stared at Jamie's gravestone. "Do you forgive me for my reckless behavior?" His eyes watered. "I am very much alone. You are in my dreams. I see you standing there, and you tell me I'm not alone."

He shook his head. "You always understood me. Even in the darkest corners of my mind, you'll be there. Give me your strength. I'm lost without you." He took a deep breath. "You keep waiting and waiting for me. I'm also waiting and thinking one day it will be time for me to join you." He shrugged as if he was apologizing. "Anyway, till next Sunday. Please know I love you and the boys very much."

Erik heard footsteps from behind, growing louder as they approached. With each step, he analyzed how they were walking. Even though Erik had been out of the game, he still had a sixth sense. The hardest part about having one's back to an approaching individual is trying to act naturally until the target is within striking distance. If they already had their sidearm drawn, it would be over in a matter of seconds. In Erik's case, he didn't mind or care if someone wanted to kill him, because if he died, he was going to see Jamie and the boys again.

He looked over his shoulder to find an elderly man in his late sixties wearing priest's attire.

"Dr. Foge," the old priest wheezed as he tried to catch his breath. "Dr. Foge, I'm so glad I caught you. The White House called. They're sending a car to pick you up." He finished just above a whisper. "Some sort of emergency."

Erik pondered why Jack would call him and what the emergency was. He glanced over the priest's shoulder at a silent stranger striding toward them, built like an ox and well-dressed in a three-piece suit, with a slight bulge under his jacket on the left side and the ideal height of a secret service agent. Then, Erik thanked the priest, who turned around and nodded to greet the young man.

"Sir," the man said, "Lancer is requesting you at the Executive Mansion."

CHAPTER 5

ANOTHER GO AROUND

"If you're prepared to adapt and learn, you can transform."
—Harry Hart, *Kingsman: The Secret Service*

Erik gestured to the secret service agent, who was a part of the Bamboo section, Presidential Motorcade, to lead the way to a 1961 Lincoln Continental four-door limousine. Upon reaching the car, the agent followed protocol, as the driver was ready to do his job. Erik saw the priest make the sign of the cross, the Holy Trinity—Father, Son, and Holy Spirit. Once the last agent got in, the three-hundred-horsepower engine, which enabled the car to accelerate from zero to sixty in approximately ten seconds, threw Erik back in his seat. The vehicle moved like a snake through the traffic on Capitol Hill. The driver came to a halt at the corner of Pennsylvania Avenue and West Executive Avenue. After a quick security check, the car could proceed and park.

The agent leaped out of the car and immediately opened Erik's door. Both men trotted up the steps, and a Marine guard snapped to attention and opened the door for them. They gave Erik a visitor's badge after he signed in. The agent, with Erik following, wove through the empty, ornate hallways of the West Wing. They displayed magnificent doorways, early American furniture, and paintings.

Jackie, the First Lady, was strolling in the distance, eyes on a piece of paper as she walked. "Morning, Floyd." She stopped and confronted Erik. "Good morning, Erik." She gracefully strolled over to greet Erik with a friendly hug and a peck on his cheek. "If you ever want to talk, I'm here for you," Jackie said with seemingly maternal concern.

Erik nodded in appreciation.

"I miss talking to Jamie in French."

He grinned and nodded again.

"Mrs. Kennedy," the Secret Service agent interrupted. "The president has requested Dr. Foge." He then stressed, "It's an urgent matter."

"Then I will walk with you." She gestured for them to continue and followed alongside as she addressed the agent. "That won't be a problem, will it, Floyd?"

"No, Mrs. Kennedy."

As they walked, Jackie handed over a paper with a list of names on it, a majority of them crossed off. Erik noticed that his name was one of them. She narrowed her eyes and said barely a whisper. "Do you notice anything?" Erik pointed to his name. She nodded and continued. "Everyone I know was crossed off, but you managed to get in." She looked for an explanation.

"Last-minute changes?" Erik smirked. He could tell she was not satisfied with his explanation as she shook her head in frustration. Erik explained, "Your definition of a party is a pure social event. However, Kenny's definition of a party is a social event intending to have people help Jack's reelection campaign in sixty-four."

Jackie's face turned bright scarlet as she stared at Erik, then she calmly changed the topic. "What did you do in the war?" She looked into Erik's eyes, which hid the things he saw.

"I'd rather not talk about it."

"You saved Jack in 1943."

Erik nodded and kept walking, then took a deep breath and slowly exhaled. "You understand the most troublesome part is I cannot tell you." He paused for a moment. "I had to work to prevent certain things, knowing that I might not come back alive to Jamie and my boys. The grim reaper was constantly looking over my shoulder, knowing I could be on the verge of death." Erik chuckled, "Sometimes, I think I survived to spite the reaper more than anything else."

They continued walking to the Oval Office as Jackie noticed children headed in her direction with chocolate smudges on their cheeks. She had a disgusted look on her face, presuming they'd been eating the candy in the Oval Office. She paused and looked at Erik, and he motioned he would solve that problem.

Once inside the president's private secretary's room, both the Secret Service agent and Jackie headed their separate ways. Erik stepped into the bustling world of Evelyn Lincoln. She organized and carried files, answered calls, took messages, and occasionally opened and shut the door to the Oval Office. She was carrying on with her normal business of the day, distracted by the papers on her desk. As Erik approached, she stood up and spoke in a delicate voice. "Erik, it's a pleasure to see you again." Her calm eyes focused on him. "He is expecting you." She gently squeezed his hand. "How are you feeling?"

Erik shrugged.

"I will be here if you need to talk."

He nodded. Muffled yelling flowed from the Oval Office. He emptied his mind of all thoughts of his personal life and prepared himself for what lay beyond.

But first, he had one more piece of pressing business to attend to. In just under a whisper, he said, "Evelyn, per Jackie, can you limit the candies the kids eat?"

She smiled and nodded.

CHAPTER 6

WHAT YOU DON'T SEE IN PANDORA'S BOX

"Spying is a like a game of chess: Sometimes you have to withdraw, sometimes you have to sacrifice one of your pieces to win."

—John Rhys-Davies

THE WHITE HOUSE, OVAL OFFICE

Jack crossed the room to shake hands with Erik. "Erik, thanks for coming. I need your help. Perhaps we can grab some lunch afterward." He pumped Erik's hand with enthusiasm, then introduced everyone. Three were familiar faces from Erik's past. "You remember Bobby?"

"Delighted to see you again. My condolences to Jamie and the boys," Bobby said as they shook hands.

Jack turned to Kenny O'Donnell.

"Thank you for coming in," Kenny said, barely controlling the resentment in his voice.

Erik shook Kenny's hand firmly and said, just above a whisper, "You know how this game is played as well as I do. Being polite won't change anything between us."

Kenny squeezed Erik's hand to make him feel uncomfortable, but Erik shook his head to say the fetal attempt didn't work.

Facing the couch to his left, Jack continued, "This is George H. Scherff, who used to be Nikola Tesla's assistant." Jack felt a strange hesitancy about what he was about to say next. "He is working on a program called Project Pegasus, dealing with time travel."

Scherff gave a conciliatory nod and offered an enigmatic grin as they shook hands. "It's been a long time, my friend. How have you been? I just heard about Jamie and the boys. You have my condolences."

Erik shrugged his shoulders as they shook hands. "I'm alive… and thank you."

"These two gentlemen are also from the ONE," Jack continued. He nodded at the older gentleman in a US Navy Commander's uniform. "This is Alan James."

Erik acknowledged the other gentleman. Erik's and Jacques Yves's eyes met with an unspoken communication.

Jack sat down at the head of the room while the others resumed their seats. Erik took one of the overstuffed chairs at the table. Jack turned to him. "Erik, I must emphasize the extreme sensitivity of this information and that it does not leave the room."

Erik nodded.

"The Nazis are placing nuclear missiles in Cuba and planning to launch an amphibious assault on the Florida coast."

Erik nodded as he glanced at Alan as if to say, *What the fuck is going on?*

Jack continued, "Mr. Scherff believes we can prevent this." Jack nodded at him, "Sir, you have our attention."

"Thank you, Mr. President." Scherff reached inside his attaché case and retrieved a manila envelope. "I can't put this delicately." He continued working on the envelope, bending up the clasp and pulling out a *New York Times* newspaper dated June 6, 1944, which he then held up. Everyone's eyes enlarged as they read the headline in bold-block letters: *ALLIED ARMIES FAIL TO LAND IN FRANCE ON THE NORMANDY COAST; GREAT LOSS OF LIFE; EISENHOWER STEPS DOWN.*

They passed the paper around the room, starting with the president, as he continued, "This headline never actually appeared in the *Times*, and forensic testing has traced the ink to a German printing press. It appears the Nazis somehow found out about D-Day in advance." Tension drained out of them instantly. Although the news was disbelieved and hushed by everyone, Erik remained neutral despite his own disbelief.

"Jesus Christ…" Kenny leaned back in his chair and looked around the room, seeing that everyone's eyes were in shock. However, Erik looked down and shook his head in disbelief.

"How in the hell did this happen?" Jack's voice communicated his disgust. The room fell silent. The President leaned back in his chair, studying the circle of men around the room, weighing them as they watched him in silence. Jack took a long, dramatic pause as he rubbed his chin, as he knew he was thinking of the imaginable: sending someone back in time to change the future.

The President leaned forward as he folded his hands on the table. "It's clear we cannot permit the Nazis to succeed." He turned to face Scherff, "Are you certain that if we use time travel, it will be possible to change history?" Scherff nodded, then Jack tapped the newspaper to emphasize his next point. "If so, we must send someone back to stop the Nazis."

Bobby looked grim as he glanced around. "I agree with the President." His young face hardened, "The person who travels back will not only have to convince our side, but if they are to trick the Nazis, they will also need to convince them."

Bobby leaned forward and stared into everyone's eyes. "How soon do we need to send someone back?"

"Two, maybe three days," Scherff replied.

"Let's make one thing clear. We need to find out who did this," Alan interjected.

"Time travel has created lots of interesting paradoxes," Erik replied in a mocking tone, receiving disgusted looks in return. "How is it that the Nazis did this?" Erik looked around the room. "Does anyone know how in the hell this happened?"

Something troubled Kenny as he stared at the blank wall and took a deep breath, "There's not a lot of time to locate someone. I agree with Erik, so let's find out how the Nazis found out." He looked each person in the eyes, making sure they understood his words without hesitation. "First, I believe we should find someone with certain qualities and expertise." Jack motioned for Kenny to continue. "They would need an extensive knowledge of D-Day, be in proper physical shape, psychologically fit, and have the right temperament."

"They'll also need to speak German fluently, with virtually no accent," Bobby added.

"Where in the hell could we find someone like this so quickly?" Jack asked, then stared at Alan. "Does ONE have anyone who fits those qualifications?"

"Mr. President, we need to look. It won't be easy." Alan glanced at Erik.

Bobby added, "Kenny and I knew a few guys from college who joined the CIA that could qualify."

"It wouldn't be so difficult if we knew how the Germans found out about D-Day," Erik interjected. "But finding the right person could take days or, in the worst-case scenario, weeks. If we 'can't figure out how the Germans learned about D-Day in advance, we will have to come up with a contingency plan for infiltrating their High Command. That individual will have to persuade them the landings will not be in Normandy."

Kenny turned to face him, using his index finger to emphasize his point. "You actually think it would be easy to approach the German High Command and convince them?"

"It might have to be as simple as that."

"Things may appear simple in your hypothetical spy world, but when we send someone back in time and actually prevent the Nazis from knowing about D-Day, they get more complex."

"Whomever we send back will be a man out of time, with no known identity," Erik explained. "Thus, neither side could identify him. In short, he would be a man that doesn't exist, and hopefully he won't be caught."

Kenny scoffed. "Are you living in a fucking spy fantasy? This isn't one of Ian Fleming's James Bond novels. We don't have an Agent 007 to solve this problem. Jesus, it feels like we've caught the Jap carriers steaming for Pearl Harbor on December 7th, ready to launch their strike on battleship row."

"I can make a few calls," Bobby suggested.

"That won't be necessary," Erik said.

"Every time we invite you to things like this, you are a pain in the ass. For once, if you cannot contribute anything useful, why don't you shut the fuck up?" Kenny barked.

"Kenny, you have misinterpreted my intentions. I haven't come here to be a thorn in your side." Erik shook his head, "Not at all. I know I'm not friendly with people, and I'm difficult."

"Jesus Christ, would you two stop this bullshit?" Jack eyed Kenny and Erik. "We need to find someone now." He turned to Bobby, "Make your calls."

"No, I know more about these kinds of operations than someone in the CIA," Erik replied.

Jack turned to him, "Erik, give me a good God damn reason why he shouldn't call."

"Who said I had a reason?"

As his hands gripped the arms of the chair, Jack squinted at

Erik and his knuckles turned white. "For as long as I've known you, you've always had a reason." He pointed at Erik. "Now, give me your fucking reason, and no bullshit."

"Because I'll do it," Erik declared. Everyone's eyes were on him. "I know it could be a suicide mission, but consider this: One, I'm knowledgeable about D-Day. Two, I'm physically fit, psychologically sound, and have the right temperament." Kenny snickered. Erik hesitated momentarily, then narrowed his eyes and focused on Kenny as he added, "I can kill you in more ways than you can think of, you son of a bitch."

Before Kenny could say a word, Alan stepped up to Erik's defense. "Kenny, I was his Chief of Station, and I can assure you not only can he fuck you up physically, but mentally as well." He nodded at Erik to continue.

"Third, and most importantly, I will give up my life if necessary."

Jack pointed at Erik. "How the hell do you know about D-Day? We met in forty-three."

"Just because I can't tell you, it doesn't mean you cannot trust me. You are just going to have to believe me."

Kenny was about to say something, but Jack motioned him to button his lips. "Erik, do you care to explain yourself?"

Erik took a deep sigh and replied. "Sometimes the only sane answer is not to answer." He leaned forward. "There are answers to your questions, but I will have to take them to my grave."

This time it was Bobby who interrupted. "Jesus Christ, guys. We are taking an enormous gamble here." He continued with disarming honesty as he glanced at Erik, "Even if you go back, there's no guarantee of success."

Kenny broke in, "This sounds more like an Ian Fleming novel." He shook his head in disbelief.

Erik waited for what he considered to be a suitable amount

of time to hear everyone's opinion, then said, "I have stopped the Germans two times working with Project Pegasus." Erik raised his hand to prevent Kenny from speaking, "I even saved a naval officer who later became president and who is one of my closest friends."

Jack glanced uncomfortably at Erik, who gave a subtle nod.

With an accusatory tone, Kenny pointed at Erik. "How in the hell did you stop the Nazis twice?" As Erik shook his head and gave his best poker face, Kenny plowed on, "Listen to me, you worthless piece of mysterious shit! I don't care if you knew Jack during the war. I asked the FBI if they have any information on you." Kenny cut his eyes at Erik as he looked at Jack, "They have nothing. Not a God damn thing!"

Scherff turned and fixed Kenny in his gaze. "Kenny, why do you think you can't find any information on him? Do you think being anonymous makes him an enemy of the State?" He shook his head and paused for a moment, "The information I and the gentlemen from ONE will give you will benefit this administration and help you be reelected for a second term."

Bobby and Jack's eyes narrowed as if they knew what the other was thinking as Scherff continued to explain, pointing at Kenny. "If you call into question what he knows, what he can verify, the data would be extraneous and be too much for you to comprehend with your limited vision." Then, Scherff looked at Jack, "Mr. President, we think bigger and further in the future than most administrations to ensure a democratic way of life."

He pointed at Erik and emphasized his last points clearly so there would not be any misinterpretation. "That man who sits in that chair has over-the-top intelligence that is beyond comprehension, and that is why he is damn good at what he does."

Bobby removed his glasses and shot Scherff a cross look, then he glanced at Erik from the corner of his eye, "What does he actually do?"

"In short, he's a ghost. You could say the ghost of the year," Scherff said.

"Do you mean a spook?" Bobby inquired. "A spy?"

Scherff nodded.

Kenny glared condescendingly at Scherff and Erik.

Scherff continued, "Have you heard of the Battle of Britain?"

Bobby nodded.

"Uranprojekt; informally known as the Uranverein?"

Bobby shook his head, looking confused.

"Forgive me, the Uranium Club?"

Bobby had a puzzled look as he glanced at Jack, who shrugged his shoulders.

Finally, Scherff explained, "It's a German nuclear weapons program."

"This is a waste of time," Kenny muttered.

Jack snapped his fingers at Kenny to keep quiet as Scherff's eyes narrowed with contempt and his face hardened, "Since you attended Harvard, I don't think you are stupid. I think you're smart enough to keep your opinions to yourself." Kenny tried to snap back, but Scherff shot him down. "Don't say a damn word. Just listen." He pointed at Erik. "Those two things would have changed the direction of the war and preventing that is exactly what he does." He paused a moment to emphasize his next point, "He works alone, with no support from anyone, including the Allies. He's willing to risk his life because he knows what he is doing is absolutely necessary. You had better take a long, hard look at him because, he is your best option to stop the Nazis." The ruthlessness of Scherff's suggestion silenced the room.

"Kenny, you should really see your face," Jacques mocked.

"Well spoken, Scherff. Kenny's expression has to put this discussion to bed," Alan added.

Jack looked around the room. "Gentlemen, I think it might be better if Erik and I will continue this conversation alone."

CHAPTER 7

COURAGE AND CONFIDENCE

"Sometimes all you need is twenty seconds of insane courage. Just, literally, twenty seconds of just embarrassing bravery. And I promise you, something great will come of it."

—Benjamin Mee, *We Bought a Zoo*

THE WHITE HOUSE

Jack acknowledged each person as they left the room. Before exiting, Scherff handed Erik the attaché case with all the information he would need for his mission. Alan said he should meet Erik at his residence later that night. Kenny left without saying goodbye. As Bobby approached, Erik held his head up, trying to conceal that he was deeply distressed.

"Bobby, relax. I've been under this kind of pressure before."

"Well, there is no expert on this subject, no wise old man that can give you advice."

Behind Erik's back, the president stared Bobby in the face, admitting he felt the same way. "As if dealing with finding out how the Nazis knew about D-Day wasn't complicated enough, you've got to worry about convincing our own side you are legit."

Erik nodded. He knew in the past that informants would

40

watch everyone and anyone that could be associated with Operation Overlord. With that in mind, he would remember that those individuals will be setting a trap, and he would be the bait.

"Bobby, when I go back in time, what keeps me going during the mission is knowing I'm fighting for something I believe in."

"Who would ever know?" Bobby turned to Jack. "Even after all these years, there is no information on him or his background. It doesn't even flag top-secret when you run his jacket. How does a guy hardly even exist in the system like that?"

"It doesn't matter to me. I'm damn happy he is working for us." Jack motioned for Erik to follow him as he strode down the plush hallway. Bobby and Erik flanked him. Instinctively, all three men assumed the same gait: confident, powerful, and no longer disoriented, knowing each had a job to do, with Secret Service agents throwing open any doors in their path. Eventually, they got to the elevator that led to the President of the United States' residence, located on the State Floor of the White House. Once the elevator doors opened, Bobby continued on his way as Erik followed Jack.

"How are you feeling?" Jack asked.

Erik shrugged.

"Erik, you can't hide your feelings from me. If you had the chance, would you go back and save Jamie?"

Erik shook his head.

"Why not?"

Jack led the way to the dining room, which was smaller and intended for more private meals than those served in the State Dining Room.

"I could go back," Erik explained, "just to see her die another way." Erik defused the conversation as he handed over Jackie's list. "We need to talk about the people Jackie wants to invite to the party."

Jack rolled his eyes.

"Listen to me… as your friend. Don't listen to Kenny about whom to invite to your parties." He pointed to his name. "He even crossed me off."

Jack nodded to say he understood the problem. "Erik, who do—or should I say, did—you work for?"

"I cannot tell you anything, or at least nothing more than you know. I am volunteering for this mission, and that's what I want you to remember if anyone asks you about me."

"Erik, I'm the President of the United States and your friend, for God's sake."

"It's going to get increasingly difficult with your advisors. They are going to ask you why you are willing to risk everything on me going back. Just let it go."

Jack's frustration grew, and he tried to plead with Erik, but the man raised his hand to prevent him from talking. "They will ask you to attack. Don't give in."

"They will ask me about you, and why I believe that sending you back in time will prevent what's happening now." Jack tossed his hands in the air. "How am I going to respond?"

"Deny everything. Time travel doesn't exist. I don't exist." Erik pointed to himself. "It will hurt when they mention my name but say you don't know me when that happens."

Jack got in Erik's face and pointed at him to get his point across. "I will not. You saved my life in 1943. You are one of my dearest and most trusted friends. Do you understand me, you son of a bitch?"

Erik nodded. "Pray for your friend," he said. "Pray I picked the right battle to win the war."

Once in the dining room, Jack told the Secret Service agents not to disturb him unless lunch came. The walls were painted a soft yellow, with yellow silk curtains tied back with ornamental cords and tassels. A series of chandeliers cast down a soft light, giving the room a calm, elegant feeling. There was a permanent installation of a late Louis XVI green marble mantel with a carved eagle and festoons in white marble. The baseboard trim was painted to match the green marble of the mantel. The Federal period dining and side chairs enhanced the room, complimented by several pieces of early nineteenth century furniture.

Jack didn't waste time. "Erik, you are telling me this goddamn time travel stuff is real?" He made hand gestures only Jack would understand as he continued. "Like H. G. Wells's novel *The Time Machine*."

"When I met Nikola Tesla in 1940, he said time travel dealt with mechanical engineering, dimensional optics, chronography, temporal paradox, and things that, to this day, I still don't understand."

The President stared at Erik with inquisitive eyes, hiding his doubt and concentrating on each word. "Are you telling me the truth?"

Without hesitation, Erik said, "Yes, Mr. President."

Jack let out a breath as he caught Erik's eyes, and his only thought was this was unbelievable.

A solid knock came at the door. It was lunch. As quickly as the serving staff arrived, they left. It was surf and turf with perfectly seasoned French fries. However, that didn't end the conversation. Between bites, Jack asked, "How many times have you been back?"

Erik took a deep breath. Before he started, he had to get Jack to keep his secret, because it could jeopardize his life. Erik used similar words in 1943, Jack recalled. "Three." Erik paused for a moment, then said in a soft voice, "My real name is Dr. Erik Függer. The CIA recruited me in 1997 as a paramilitary operations officer, and later I was a senior analyst. They introduced me to Project Pegasus in 2008, and that was the first time I traveled back in time."

Jack took a sip of wine and tried to hide his shock. "Do you like it?"

Erik shook his head. "Sometimes I feel like I am damned." He paused for a long time before continuing. "In a sense, traveling back to the past feels like entering a dream world or paralleling our own Earth's time and space. I have a wealth of another kind, my knowledge of history and things I learned while working with the CIA." Erik shook his head and grinned. "I have taken on many roles. They placed me at pivotal junctures during World War Two because people continually are trying to alter its course." He finished his wine. "Sometimes, I feel like the greatest actor of the twentieth century, as if I am being tested with the ability to respond to the challenge of preserving the timeline."

"That's an interesting way of saying what you do," Jack said. "I have a question."

Erik nodded.

"What do they write about me in the future? Will they reelect me in sixty-four?"

Erik said nothing as he breathed calmly.

"Well?"

"Well, what?"

"Are you able to tell me?"

Erik took a deep sigh and shook his head.

"Why not? If I can learn from my mistakes, I can make this country better for future generations."

"Some things are better left unknown until the time is right."

Jack shook his head and motioned for Erik to give him a better answer.

"One could say I am like God. I go through my life knowing that horrible acts in history will happen, and I do nothing."

"You self-righteous son of a bitch. But you will travel back in time to change the past."

"Don't make me regret telling you about this." Erik stood up and stuck his finger in Jack's face. "I'll tell you this…" He leaned forward. "If I won't travel back to save Jamie and my boys, I'll be damned if I reveal anything about your future." Erik took his seat and continued, "I'm a military historian and know the pitfalls of meddling with history in times of crisis. There's no doing things half-assed, and if I don't fix it without an eye to the future, there will be no future… or a future we don't recognize."

"Alan told me you were like an ocean—deep and mysterious, yet you are incredibly dangerous to underestimate."

Even though Erik was no longer working for the intelligence community, there were certain things he still remembered: it was part acting, part strategy, and, most importantly, being a sponge and listening.

Jack continued, "He also said most people think they know you through and through, but only see the side you allow them to see." Jack leaned back in his chair and studied Erik's body language for a moment before he continued. "Jamie was right. You build walls around you, you don't let many people in, and they have to gain your trust. You are much smarter than most." Jack pointed to emphasize his next words. "Whenever someone underestimates you, you prove them wrong." Jack grinned as he thought he had figured out his friend.

Erik added with a cunning grin, "I don't get angry often, but when I do, fear my wrath because I'm both holy water and hell fire."

Jack gulped as a chill shot up his spine that caused him to get goosebumps. He leaned forward and folded his hands on the table. "Is it easy to kill someone?"

Erik shook off the question. "As an operative, I try to avoid confrontation and use lethal force only when necessary." He chuckled as he continued, "I can kill a person thirty different ways with my bare hands, and if you think that's something," he smirked, "you should see what I can do with a toothbrush."

"How many people have you killed?"

"Three hundred and twenty-six," he replied coldly, without remorse.

Jack raised his hands to signal he had heard enough and wanted to change the topic. "Erik, we need to find someone else who has the same qualifications."

Erik shook his head, but Jack didn't stop.

"Listen to me, damn it. It is not only a request from a friend but a direct order from the President of the United States."

Erik pulled his shoulders close to his body, arms crossed, as he tilted his head and narrowed his eyes.

"Erik, this is not your job anymore. Haven't you already done enough?"

"Jack, I can handle this. I have to go back. There is no one else more qualified for this, and we don't have time to waste."

"Erik, why are you doing this?"

"Because I'm the best option we have."

Jack looked on for more explanation.

"Even with all the training, few expected I'd survive my first mission." Erik's face twitched as he continued, "Before I was sent back, I was told only a few guys in the agency succeeded. I was one of them. Then I did it again, and again." Erik drew Jack closer with every word that was spoken. "Jack, I know you don't want me to go, but it is something I need to do."

Jack met Erik's eyes and reached out his hand to him. They shook hands as soldiers and friends.

CHAPTER 8

THE TEST THAT STUMPED THEM ALL

"I figure if there's a God, He won't mind,
considering the situation I'm in."

—Andy Weir, *The Martian*

KENNEDY WARREN, WASHINGTON D.C.

The hum of the ceiling fan's motor consumed the room. A single light on the desk broke the darkness, dissipating over classified documents—draft cables and memorandums from Operation Overlord. Erik leaned back in his chair, studying a few photographs. He tossed them on the desk and swiveled around to the nearest bookcase to reach for two huge three-ring binders titled *United States Army in World War II: The War Department: Operation Overlord.*

Erik hunched over his desk, rubbing his fingers through his hair. His notebook, filed with documentation from various sources, sat open beside him. He was perplexed by the days between May 15, 1944 in London to D-Day on June 6, 1944. After pushing a series of pages of dossiers, he whacked his forehead, hoping some information would leap out to help him. Jacques walked into the office and Erik looked up sheepishly.

"Does it help when you do that?"

Erik spared him a glance.

"Coffee?" Jacques took a sip.

"Just throw it in my eyes. It'll work faster."

Jacques fell into a chair, clearly grappling with Erik's frustration as he continued. "I'm close to finding the answer."

"This close, huh?" Jacques said, joking as he gestured an inch with his thumb and index finger.

"Shut up," Erik replied as they both chuckled. "Do you ever feel like everything you do doesn't make a difference? You travel back in time and fix history, and then someone else fucks with it again. You fix it again, and the cycle repeats itself."

Jacques displayed an elaborate hand gesture, as if he were trying to wrap his mind around the concept. "Doesn't that drive you crazy, that you make a difference only to find out that sometimes it doesn't make a difference because something else happens?"

"Well, one could describe me as Sam Beckett or say that I love insanity."

Jacques rubbed his chin as if he was deep in thought, then pointed at Erik. "Both."

Erik nodded. "I know I repeated the same thing at different times in World War Two. It was then that I expected and hoped they would learn not to change the past, seeing that it never ends well. You can call me a fool or one of the maddest men for what I'm doing." Erik shook his head. "I always think about how much worse it would be if I hadn't succeeded."

"You're talented at putting right what once went wrong in the war, but when are you going to learn that someone else will need to do it?"

"Where's Scherff and Alan?"

Jacques checked his watch, acknowledging the same feeling. "They should be here any minute."

Erik nodded and shifted back to analyzing the documents. Despite the chemistry of his friends, acting like an intelligence team at Langley made them seem to miss their third wheel, Scherff and Alan. Both men looked up as they heard the front door creaking open.

"Where the hell are you?" A deep, commanding voice barreled out. Erik and Jacques heard Alan out in the hall, and the tension drained out of them instantly.

"In here!" Erik declared. They turned to the door as Alan and Scherff entered the office. Both men took a seat. All grappled with their own disbelief and were hushed as if they were trying to find a needle in a haystack.

"Jesus Christ, guys. What the hell? Please tell me you found something." Alan motioned at the clutter on the desk. "Have you discovered anything yet?" He picked up a few of the draft cables and browsed through them. "Did you have any idea of who is behind this?" Alan turned to Scherff. "Any possible warnings or sense of motivation?"

Scherff shook his head. "There's something more significant than motivation. How did the Nazis find out? And, who helped them?" All four men seemed confused and doubtful, yet hopeful that something might come to light. When did the Germans find out about D-Day? He added. "Our analysis showed the Nazis never infiltrated the network of Operation Overlord."

"We all know Von Rundstedt ran the entire show." Erik strode around the office. "Hitler listened only to him." Erik grabbed a map of the Normandy Coast and opened it to full length as he placed it on the desk. "He had sixty divisions, but only nine in Normandy." Erik took a deep breath as he added grimly. "In Pas de Calais, there were over three hundred thousand men, who in this timeline are waiting for our troops in Normandy."

The room fell silent as Erik strode around his desk to his chair, sat down, and pulled documents toward him.

Alan glared at Erik from across the room. "Did you find out how long it took the Germans to move their units from Calais to Normandy?"

Erik leaned over and flipped through, skimming over the documents. "Less than thirty hours."

Alan's face was set like stone. "How many people knew about the landings?"

Erik turned his eyes inward, remembering, but Scherff interjected. "We are uncertain." He pointed at the large stack of documents that added to the conversation. "Of all the documents we found, there were only a few of the individuals who knew."

Erik rummaged in the top drawer of his desk for a few moments, then pulled out a small, white card. He lifted the telephone and dialed the number on the card. The phone rang and was picked up on the third ring.

"Jack, sorry to bother you, but I need some information from the meeting earlier today." Erik cupped the receiver and whispered to the others to get ready to go for dinner. "Okay, I need the dossiers of all those who knew about Operation Overlord and their current whereabouts." Erik rubbed his fingers through his hair. "Jack, I realize that information is still Top Secret. Don't tell me you can't do it, because I am confident you can. And don't tell me you won't do it, because I've got to have it. I need to know, and I need to know now, or we will have the Germans either invade us or use their A10 rockets armed with atomic warheads."

Erik glanced at his pocket watch and nodded. "Perfect. I will stop by and pick them up." Erik set the phone in its cradle and walked out of his office without looking back. He motioned the others to follow and said, "Let's hope I'm right. We'll find out in a few hours."

CHAPTER 9

FINDING THE ANSWER IS JUST THE BEGINNING

"For a spy, the strain of a deep cover assignment goes beyond just being alone, surrounded by enemies who'd kill you if they knew your identity. If you want to survive, you can't let any of that strain show."

— *Burn Notice*, "Nature of the Beast"

KENNEDY WARREN, WASHINGTON D.C.

"All right, gentlemen. Let's take our seats," Erik said once they were back in his office. Everyone did so. "If we're hoping to find the answer to how the Germans found out about D-Day, let's discuss the facts we know."

Erik looked around the room. Some of them looked as if they were racking their brains. Alan nodded slowly and replied. "We know it happened between May 31 and June 4, since it took the Germans less than thirty hours to move their forces from Pas de Calais to Normandy."

Scherff interrupted, "All right, my history is foggy." He pounded his forehead with the palm of his hand. "I remember hearing something like a D-Day incident."

"An incident?" Jacques asked. He looked up at Erik, who stood up as if waiting for a reply. "Erik, do you know what he's talking about?"

Erik shook his head as Alan reached for his drink, knocking the dossiers off the desk. Erik motioned Jacques to a bookcase. "What are we looking for?"

Alan sounded flustered. "Well, I am certain we will find it." He placed several dossiers on the desk. "I know it. We will find it when we least expect it. I…" Alan fumbled over his thoughts and words. "What I meant was." He dismissed the subject completely, rubbed his hands together, and leaned over as something caught his eye.

"Major General Henry JF Miller." Everyone turned to Alan for an explanation. "It says that in May of 1944, while attending a dinner party at The Fumoir, located in Claridge, in London, he leaked the date of the upcoming Operation Overlord during a conversation with a fellow officer, saying that 'the invasion will come on June 6."

"That could be the starting point," Jacques suggested, pointing at information he was reviewing in a book. "You know, there is testimony here stating when news of this security breach reached Eisenhower, Miller was demoted to lieutenant colonel and sent home. Eisenhower mentioned in Miller's dossiers that he was more useful back home, and they did not need his skills in the European theater."

"Well, it doesn't prove anything. It's just part of the picture," Scherff pointed out.

"The Nazis must have learned from that," Alan said with a sigh as Jacques shook his head. "What do you mean, no?" Alan snapped as he crossed his arms and stood. "You just told us about Miller's mouth; that's how the Nazis found out."

"Alan, that happened in both timelines. It's not something new," Erik said. Erik grabbed Miller's dossier, skimmed it, and repeated what he read. "Eisenhower said, 'He was more useful back home, and we did not need his skills in the European theater.' Eisenhower ordered him to be en route within twenty-four hours."

"I am not following you," Alan muttered, rocking on his heels. When he noticed everyone staring at him, he sat down with his fists clenched in frustration.

"We all agree that the Germans took less than thirty hours to move the bulk of their forces from Pas de Calais to Normandy?" Erik looked around the room, and everyone nodded, then glanced down at the dossier. "They sent Miller home on the thirty-first of May, and the Germans moved their forces on the fourth of June, so something happened within those four days."

"All right. Let's talk about it." Alan conceded. "There's something in front of us, but we aren't seeing it."

"Jack said these," Erik placed his hand on the dossiers, "are the only individuals that knew every detail about Operation Overlord." He removed Miller's dossier.

"Do you think you will find the answer in them?" Scherff asked.

"There's nothing in these reference books," Jacques motioned to Erik's library. Then he pointed at the binder detailing the plans for Operation Overlord, which was in front of Erik. "Did you find anything?"

Erik shook his head. "No. And I'm not sure the dossiers will have the answer. I'm saying that it's *possible* the answer could be in them."

Jacques hinted, "So, what are we looking for?" There was a long silence, and suddenly everyone looked at Erik as Jacques forewarned, "We could be here all night."

"Look, gentlemen," Erik asserted. "We are looking for a needle in a haystack." He leaned back in his chair. "This is an extremely crucial thing to remember. The smallest detail could be the answer we are searching for."

"We are trying to find a needle with an eye among the other needles," Scherff added.

They divided the remaining dossiers, with each examining one closely, analyzing every detail. Then, one by one, the dossiers were thrown back toward the center of the desk. With the pile getting larger, frustration was building, with some making jerky movements and others clasping their hands behind their backs.

"Does anyone think there isn't a chance we will find anything?" Scherff asked.

"I don't know about anyone else, but most of these guys are retired," Jacques revealed, with the others nodding in agreement.

"It doesn't seem unreasonable to think we might find something in here," Erik replied, trying to hide his doubts as the situation in front of him looked bleak.

"You are asking us," Jacques said, "to find something that might not exist in these dossiers, or we might never find or know how the Germans found out about D-Day, on nothing but a whim."

"Maybe we'll learn something we don't know. It's not a sure thing, but there is a chance."

"If we don't find anything," Alan said as he tossed another dossier on the pile, "then what do you plan on doing?"

There was a long, awkward pause as Erik glanced around the table. He got up silently, strode over, looked at a picture of Jamie, and heard her in his head. *Erik, you are so strong and true. I still believe in you.* As the others waited intently, he turned around. "I was just thinking that perhaps there's a possibility we might consider tricking the Germans about D-Day."

Erik paused for a moment as he pulled a book from the shelf and flipped the pages until he came upon the information he was looking for. "The Germans knew Patton's First Army was heading their way because of their spy working in New York. There was an operative working under the alias Albert Van Loop. He had become a double agent for the Federal Bureau of Investigation. In September of 1943, he used the codes our German intelligence service supplied to inform us that divisions were embarking from New York, bound for the British Isles."

Alan uttered. "Do you mean to suggest?"

"Yes," Erik replied, as Jacques looked baffled. "Just like the O.G.D.S. days."

Scherff was focused on a dossier and seemed to be suddenly interested in something he just read. "Oh, my dear God." The room became quiet. "This is not good."

"What is it?" Alan demanded.

"On May 29, 1944, Major Ronnie Schan left the Iroquois Hotel for LaGuardia Airport. He was General Miller's replacement as chief intelligence officer since his other one died in a plane crash." Scherff looked up as the blood drained from his face. One by one, everyone gulped. "He disappeared on June 1, never to be seen or heard from again." He pulled a photo from the dossier. "Erik, he looks like you."

Alan asked, "How are you going to find this guy?"

"I could start with very light surveillance at the hotel," Erik suggested. "First, I will be his babysitter. I will back off. I will act like I am a part of the OSS."

Jacques shook his head. "Sadly, I don't think that would solve the problem." Erik motioned him to continue. "You cannot just watch him. If they kidnap him, they won't need you and will kill you. Find some different way." Jacques paused for a moment. "You may have to kill him." Jacques read Erik's face. "Does this discourage you?"

"Erik, I agree with Jacques, but how would you get rid of the body?" Alan added, and Erik shrugged his shoulders.

Scherff gasped. "Are you saying he needs to be murdered?" Alan nodded. "My God, how can you justify murder?"

"As Mr. Spock said on Star Trek, the needs of the many out-weigh the needs of the few, or the one," Erik replied.

"Erik, are you sure you will be able to do this?" Alan asked as he cocked his head toward Erik's expressionless face. A pair of tense blue eyes stared back at him. Alan could read Erik's mind and knew he was focused on solving the problem.

Erik considered everything he needed to do, including murdering Major Ronnie Schan. Not only that, if the Germans kidnapped him, what would they possibly do to him? And how would he find Schan then?

Alan crossed his arms against his chest and continued to look at Erik.

Erik said, "If I wasn't willing to risk my life for other lives…" He thought for a moment. "Well, I guess I wouldn't be effective at my job." Erik stood in front of everyone and declared. "It can be done."

CHAPTER 10

SENSING ELEMENTS

"I love rumors! Facts can be so misleading, where rumors, true or false, are often revealing."

—Hans Landa, *Inglorious Basterds*

SS HEADQUARTERS, BERLIN, GERMANY, MAY 26, 1944

Two twenty by thirty-five centimeter, rectangle pennants in black and white, diagonally divided and surrounded by a silver stripe, bearing the SS-eagle in silver in the center, fluttered over a black Mercedes-Benz 770 W150 as it pulled in front of the main entrance of SS Headquarters. A sentry opened the rear door and stood waiting. A man stepped out with a collar insignia that read RFSS: Reichsführer der SS, Himmler's personal staff.

The man might have stepped straight off an SS parade ground with his crisp, immaculate black uniform, officer's cap, and polished jackboots. The uniform had enormous importance, obliterating individuality and representing the hierarchical order of society while manifesting the encompassing power of the party and state. He had an innate sense of superiority, especially when he wore his uniform. He was a colonel of the Sicherheitsdienst des Reichsführer-SS security service, or SD, with the ribbons of the SS Long Service Award and the NSDAP Long Service, and a Knight's Cross at his throat. He had a striking, handsome, yet enigmatic appearance; however, he had an expressionless, pale face that enhanced his unemotional, cobalt eyes that were fixed and staring.

If he were not walking, one might assume he was a corpse, had it not been for the subtle blinking of his eyes. His name was Apophis Adelram. Just like in Egyptian mythology, Apophis threatened the underworld and symbolized evil. All those who met or knew him felt threatened and feared him. His demeanor was cold but warm, precise but fluid, and ruthless but charming. However, with all those qualities, he was relaxed and calculated and did everything with Rolex watch precision. He exemplified Nazi and Aryan ideology, being a shrewd and merciless SS officer.

He had been called to SS Headquarters to fulfill another objective by his Führer. Like every other previous objective he had achieved before, Apophis followed his orders to the letter in order to ensure his place in the SD hierarchy. He marched with purpose, his footsteps echoing through the numerous security checkpoints throughout the cavernous hallways. Adelram had a willful mind and a commanding set of unwavering opinions, both strengthened by the SS ideology.

Himmler sensed Apophis's ambition in the SS because of his powerful personality, which was well-suited for leadership. He had a long, suspenseful walk ahead of him, but was getting closer to his meeting with Heinrich Himmler, Reichsführer of the dreaded SS, who would ask him many direct questions about allied landings, which he was prepared to answer.

He approached the final threshold to Himmler's office. Outside was a secretary who picked up a receiver, said a few words, hung it up, and stood. Armed sentries stood on either side of the door. Apophis paused with a certain level of uncertainty but knew he could overcome any obstacle. He turned to face the secretary, who saluted with the phrase that always follows: "Heil Hitler."

Apophis reciprocated the greeting back to the secretary.

"Your pistol, please, Herr Colonel." The secretary said with his hand extended toward Apophis. He removed his Walther P38 from its holster and he handed it over, and they placed it in a locked drawer. With a nod to the secretary, the man opened the door.

Apophis squared his shoulders as he entered the office of Himmler. The walls were matte white, accented with polished brass, triple-armed candelabra wall sconces placed strategically throughout that cast soft, ambient light over the large area. The room had a beautiful, polished brass chandelier trimmed with high-quality crystals that created a uniformity of sparkle, light reflection, and spectral colors. It was characteristic of the grand chandeliers which decorated the finest chateaux and palaces across Europe and reflected a time of class and elegance. A portrait of the Führer hung on the wall.

Reichsführer Himmler, an incongruously petite man with slicked back, neatly combed brown hair, cold hazel eyes behind circular, steel-rimmed glasses, and a black SS Reichsführer uniform, sat in an oversized chair with a tall back behind a huge desk, writing as always. Bundles of manila folders were stacked neatly in front of him, along with many rubber stamps he had the authority to use. Himmler placed his pen on the desk, stood, and saluted the colonel, who did the same, but the gesture was almost casual. Between the two men of unquestionable loyalty to the Reich, they were merely going through the motions. Both men took their seats.

Himmler scrutinized Apophis as he pulled his dossier from a drawer. From a quick skim, he learned his family thought his joining the SS would bring great shame to their noble name. This constantly put him at odds, especially with his father. When he was an SS recruit, he was strong and willful. Himmler and his superiors noticed he had two amazing traits: one, an exceptional intellect, and two, the ability to manipulate people to get what he wanted, which was helpful with interrogations. He used those skills to advance within the SS ranks.

"You'll forgive me, Herr Colonel. Reports have been coming at all hours of the day about cowards in the Wehrmacht who would stand up against the Reich and the Führer." He removed his glasses and continued, firmly emphasizing his next point as he handed a folder to Apophis. "I need you to find out information on the exact location of the allied invasion."

Himmler waited until Apophis skimmed the documents and photographs before he continued. "We learned the First United States Army Group is heading to England from our spy working in New York. Albert Van Loop is the alias used by our operative. He became a double agent inside the Federal Bureau of Investigation, and in September of last year, he used the codes supplied by our intelligence service to inform us that divisions were embarking at New York, bound for the British Isles."

Apophis lifted a photo and asked, "So, they gave Patton command of FUSAG?"

Himmler nodded.

"They say his troops nicknamed him blood and guts."

Himmler nodded again, then added, "He is a consummate leader and a brilliant tactician." He pulled out and unfolded a map of southeast England and pointed at it with a pen. "Eisenhower stationed him and FUSAG in Kent."

Apophis rubbed his chin. "Do we know FUSAG's strength?"

"So far, our sources tell us it comprises the Third American Army and has the 31st Corps and the US 33rd Corps. Those will join with other Allied forces, and we believe they will land in the

Pas de Calais region, north of the river Seine, where the English Channel is narrowest. It will be your responsibility to confirm this and determine further details."

"Is that the bulk of their forces?" Apophis asked.

Himmler shook his head as he pointed to a cable dated May 20, 1944. "America is going to have fifty more divisions once the beachhead is established."

Apophis raised an eyebrow in a questioning slant.

Himmler circled the area around Norwich on the map. "We had to move the Thirteenth Signal Intelligence Battalion, which supports the Fifteenth Army, to Dieppe because there is a large amount of communication traffic in that area."

Himmler leaned back in his chair. "I spoke to Field Marshal General Sperrle, who commands the Third Luftflotte. He advised me it is hopelessly weakened by half-trained pilots, and their aircraft are exposed to constant attacks by the Allied air forces, on the ground and in the air. So, he can provide limited air reconnaissance."

He adjusted his glasses, leaned forward, and pointed to emphasize his next words. "Colonel Adelram, I have called you because what you need to do is of critical importance to the Reich." He paused and picked up the telephone but didn't dial. Instead, he disconnected the line. When he was certain the line was dead, he continued. "Is The Royal Botanical Garden Society still in London?"

Adelram nodded. The Royal Botanical Garden Society was a front for a very successful Fifth Columnist. They were the last since MI5 had rounded up the lot by December 1939.

"Herr Colonel, what is the latest from the horticulturists?"

"They believe they have discovered one of the allied hubs where they are discussing their invasion." This drew Himmler in. "They have seen several high-ranking British, Canadian, and American officers entering The Royal Historic Conservatory on Matthew Parker Street." Apophis, who liked to consider himself a man of action, sighed inwardly and looked into Himmler's eyes. "We know, from our sources, that American officers eat at Fumoir, a restaurant at Claridge's in London. We will follow one who holds the rank of major or colonel and kidnap and interrogate him."

A sadistic grin appeared on Himmler's face as he replied. "I admire your ability to innovate."

Apophis nodded in appreciation.

"It is for that reason that I assigned you to SS interrogations."

Apophis knew Himmler also appreciated his use of his knowledge as a medical doctor and his desire to experiment on prisoners of war as a ruthless tool whenever the Reich needed information it could use to further their plans. Furthermore, Apophis demonstrated a mastery of the art of diplomacy and conversation in his interrogation techniques.

He inferred the state of mind of his subjects, reading the individual and using the surrounding environment to his advantage before acting. When interrogating prisoners, he showed profound restraint and patience, and he kept his darkness hidden until he knew exactly when to torture them. In addition, he never chose random methods. Learning what his victim feared the most often led to a more efficient process. His ruthless and relentless determination made him a truly otherworldly enigma, a monster of warped principles who employed any means necessary to get the information he needed.

Himmler stood behind his desk, removed his silver pince-nez with meticulously polished lenses. He looked sternly into Apophis's eyes. "I'm putting you in command of our intelligence services. I don't care how you get the individuals who know about the allied landings or the methods you used to interrogate them. Torment and control them. They are to be treated as the untermensch or race traitors they are to find out where the landings will take place."

To Apophis, his victims were nothing more than a mind to break and a well from which he could draw information. He stood at attention, clicked his heels, saluted, and stated, "It will be done."

CHAPTER 11

PREPARING FOR THE JOURNEY TO A VACANT LIFE

"Now, this war will be fought on the battlefield, but make no mistake that peace will be won with brains, not brawn."

— *Manhattan*, Season 1, Episode 1

HIDDEN MEADOW APARTMENTS, COLORADO SPRINGS, COLORADO

Erik stood in front of the mirror in a United States Army olive drab dress uniform. The rank insignia on the shoulder lapels identified him as a major, and ribbons representing the American Campaign Medal, Soldier's Medal, Legion of Merit, and Distinguished Service Medal were pinned on the upper left breast of the jacket. He had an officer's wool service cap, olive drab, with a russet-brown leather visor, two polished brass buttons that held the chin strap, and a polished brass United States eagle crest on the peak. The final touch to the uniform were polished Army-issue, russet leather Oxford shoes and brown socks.

Erik took a deep breath as he assessed his abilities and the odds of a successful mission. He closed his eyes and saw a different scene from a different time, 1944, when Jamie was alive, and he was preparing to go to Berlin to save Hitler. A faint smile came to his face when he remembered how Jamie's perfume smelled as it drifted between them. Her innocent face had water in her eyes as she looked him over like a drill sergeant during a uniform inspection.

She tried to contain her tears as she stepped forward, adjusted his lapel, and brushed something off his shoulder. Tears trickled down her face as he reached out, slowly lifted her head, and kissed her gently. He wiped her tears away and stared into her eyes.

Jacques's voice dissolved the memory.

"One or two fingers?" Jacques sat behind him with two glasses and a bottle of Red Label. Erik exhaled as his eyes slowly focused on his reflection in the mirror. For the first time, he saw the look he gave Jamie every time he had to go away. Erik uttered to her memory, "I promise I'll be back." That time, though, she would not be waiting. Nor did he know if he would ever come back.

Erik turned to face Jacques and motioned for him to continue.

"The fact is that you're used to doing this sort of thing—putting right what went wrong in World War Two. I know you'll be able to do your part when the time comes." Jacques lifted his glass. "To your determination."

Erik raised his glass and added, "Actually, it is called stress-inoculation resilience." They both took a sip. "I can think of no other profession where I can travel back in time to historical events and meet people I read about in history books and use my talents as a Paramilitary Operations Officer to preserve history as we know it." He shook his head and chuckled. "And have people try to kill me who altered history to suit their own twisted vision of how things should have gone."

Jacques stood up and cupped his hands over Erik's shoulders. "I know it's tough cleaning up after people's mistakes in history. The reason I admire you for doing this job is your tenacity. I'm sure it will eat away at you until there's nothing left." He took a deep sigh. "However, every time, I feel as though you will never return. It makes me nervous."

There was a solid knock on the door, which opened abruptly, revealing a sentry. "Sir, they are ready for you."

The sentry escorted them outside. At first glance, the building they were leaving looked like part of a typical apartment complex with manicured lawns and landscapes, a private, gated pool and hot tub, a dozen apartment buildings, a leasing office, and a clubhouse. However, this was just a front for preying eyes. The manicured lawns and landscapes hid antennas, microwave relay systems, and security cameras. Surrounding the complex was a ten-foot-high, chain-link fence topped with razor wire and patrolled by armed guards. They were in the heart of Hidden Meadow Apartments, home of Project Pegasus and ONE.

The sentry led them to another building, where armed guards verified their identifications. Once inside, there were more armed guards. A man behind a nondescript desk stood up as they entered and said, "Identify yourselves." One by one, Erik and the others offered their ID cards and clearance papers. Even with all that, one had to remember a pass phrase before they could continue.

The man said out of the blue, "The snow this year is better at Howelsen Hill."

Without hesitation, Erik replied, "Not better than Ski Broadmoor."

After that, the man pulled out a brass key and inserted it into a control panel in the wall behind the desk. Wood panels on the walls slid apart to reveal an elevator, and the armed guards moved to the back of the car, followed by Erik and Jacques. After a short ride down, the elevator came to a halt and the doors opened. They were met by another pair of sentries and an officer.

The officer stepped forward and asked Jacques. "AC or DC?"

"AC."

"Why?"

"Because it can be converted to different voltages relatively easily."

The officer motioned them to follow down a long corridor, then turned to lead them through several hallways with security cameras and warning signs announcing a restricted area appeared with increasing frequency. At the end of one corridor, they came upon a heavily armored door flanked by guards and a security camera focused on those entering and exiting. The officer swiped his identification card and punched in a six-digit security code. A buzzer sounded, and they entered the heart of Project Pegasus.

A scene of such technological splendor greeted Jacques that for several minutes he stood speechless, just like the first time he saw it in 2012. The enormous room, approximately three stories tall and two hundred yards long, dazzled his eyes. He took everything in as he mouthed, *oh my god*. Erik glanced around, remembering the last time he was there, in 1943.

"This reminds me of NASA's mission control room when I first saw it," Jacques whispered as he nodded at the eight rows of adjoining, nearly identical workstations with one or two computer screens, a keyboard, and an assortment of switches, buttons, and dials.

As in 2012, technicians and work crews were busy checking and rechecking vital systems. Jacques turned to look twenty feet above them when Erik grabbed his attention. Well-armed guards in black body armor carrying high-caliber weapons walked up and down a catwalk that covered the full length of the room. Their eyes were fully alert, watching every inch of the control room.

Then Erik pointed down, and Jacques was amazed as he noticed the floor was clear like glass, with pull-back panels and, beneath that, different-sized bundles of multi-colored cables branching out and twisting like the root system of an oak tree.

The cables merged into several large groups as they approached the gray concrete wall at the far end of the room. A single black door sat in the center of the wall. Erik advised Jacques it was the entrance to the time machine. Words on the floor in bright, blocky red lettering read,

DANGER: RADIATION
ONLY TRAVELERS AND AUTHORIZED
PERSONNEL BEYOND THIS POINT

From the organized chaos, Alan and Scherff appeared with warm but concerned smiles. Although Erik was focused and attentive, part of his mind was going over the plan to meet and kill Ronnie Schan. As before, he would be alone, traveling back to a dangerous period of time. He was going to be a man who did not exist on a crusade to preserve history and do whatever is necessary to put what went wrong right. Again, as so many times before, one man really could make a difference.

"Are you ready?" Scherff asked.

"Kinda, sorta, maybe, but not quite." Erik lowered his eyes. Then, with a deep breath, he nodded, signaling he was ready.

"They will notice any slip in character. It would be lethal. I cannot stress this enough," Alan said.

Erik nodded again.

"You have one objective," Alan added. "You know what it is."

Erik's tense blue eyes looked back at him with the extra seriousness they held when his mind was focused on the mission.

Scherff took out a pen, scribbled on a notepad, and handed it to Erik. "Here is the information about Ronnie. Oh, and don't get caught murdering him."

"Understood. Will the OSS report him missing?"

Alan shook his head. "Because of national security, they won't let that information out on an open circuit because they don't know who is listening." He pointed at Erik to emphasize his next point. "Despite that, make sure they can't find or identify the body."

Alan and Erik shook hands. "You better get moving, my friend. Remember to use this." Alan tapped the side of his head. "If you get captured, your brain might be the only weapon you have."

"Good luck, my friend. I will be waiting for you in 1944," Scherff added.

"So, until I see you again," Jacques said, hiding his doubt. "Here is a little something." He placed several paperclips in Erik's hand. "Never know when you will need them. Keep them in a safe place."

"Thanks," Erik said.

"Don't make me come back and wrap you in a flag."

"I don't plan on dying."

"I understand, but shit happens."

Erik nodded. "See you in a few days."

"I'll see you in a few seconds."

"I'll not forget you, Jacques." Erik gave Jacques a brotherly hug.

The black door slid open, revealing a stark white hallway. Erik walked to the end and entered a circular room. He took deep breaths as he prepared himself for what would come next. The room filled with a hum that sounded like electronic bees. Erik could never get used to that part. The noise consumed the room and grew louder by the second, assaulting his eardrums. Then, a blinding, bluish-white light, coming from nowhere and everywhere at once, filled the room. A chill swept through his body. Finally, Erik felt as if he was falling. He screamed as he was transported back to the 1940s for the third time.

Jacques turned to Alan. "Do you think he has a chance of succeeding?"

Alan nodded. "Erik is the best at what he does. If anybody has a chance, it's him."

"What if the SS captures him?" Scherff asked.

"I don't know, and I don't know what they will do to him." Alan turned to face them. "If he does get captured, he will do anything to confuse the Nazis to make them think the landing will be at Pas de Calais. As long as there's a single breath in his body, he will not give up until they think that."

CHAPTER 12

ONE LIFE TO LOSE

"What is food to one, is to others bitter poison."
— Lucretius, Roman philosopher

NEW YORK CITY, NEW YORK, MAY 27, 1944

Erik always hated the effects of time travel. He never got used to it. He tried to stand, took a deep breath, and slowly exhaled. That didn't help, because he still stumbled forward as if he were drunk. Like the last three times he came back, he opened his eyes but saw only a blur. His eyes adjusted and his surroundings slowly came into focus, but the world felt as if it had flipped upside down.

He took a quick glance to make sure no one saw him and scoped out the surrounding terrain. There were grassy swards, gentle slopes, and shady glens, as well as steep and rocky ravines. There were sidewalks lined with lamp posts covering the entire space and blending into the landscape, and there was a subtle chatter of people walking along. He got to the highest point he could find and studied the buildings around him as he conducted his analysis. He realized he was in Central Park in New York City.

As he made his way out of the park, he looked for a cop and asked for his help to find the Iroquois Hotel and a florist. Erik was in luck and found one and got the information he needed. The Iroquois Hotel is an eighteen-minute walk from 59th Street, on West 44th Street. The first step was the florist. Exiting the park on 59th Street was like stepping into a blender with every ingredient known to humanity tossed in. Crossing the street was like the video game Frogger, but a lot more dangerous since people didn't know how to drive. The most effective solution was to go with a crowd of people crossing the street. However, that guaranteed nothing because it ended up being like Darwin's Theory of Natural Selection. Erik remembered it was like that when he was there in 1940, but it seemed worse.

He headed down 6th Avenue, lined with taxis parked with their headlights on, waiting for their next customer. Rumbling cars were joined by the occasional iron horseshoe stomping on the pavement. The sidewalks were filled with people who kept to themselves in their own isolated world. As he continued to move into the heart of New York, a cacophony of odors and sounds bombarded his senses. Car exhaust, intoxicating perfumes, colognes, horse manure, and those who hadn't taken a shower attacked his nostrils. Squealing brakes, blaring horns, and other ear-piercing noises echoed off the surrounding buildings.

He glanced at his watch; it was nearly four o'clock. Ronnie Schan should be checking in at five o'clock in room 627. Erik was hoping there was a room next to his that wasn't taken. But only time would tell. As the sun dipped lower, the vivid colors of the city gradually faded into a dull gray. The temperature dropped a little in the short time he was there. There was a slight chill in the air, but it was pleasant outside.

Erik finally made it to 44th Street and turned left. He mentally prepared how he would meet and interact with Ronnie and get close enough to put VISINE eye drops from 2021, which Alan gave him, in his drink. A medical doctor briefed him before he went back that the tetrahydrozoline in the eye drops would cause blurred vision, headache, and a fast heart rate, just to name a few. A doorman greeted Erik and asked if he needed help with his bag. Erik kindly refused. He then crossed the lobby, walked up to the registration desk, and was greeted warmly.

"Good afternoon. Can I help you?" the clerk asked.

"I'd like a room, please. I would prefer a room on the sixth floor if that's possible, and do you have a room close to 627? My friend is staying in that room."

The clerk responded with a smile. "We have room 628, across from Mr. Schan's room." He reached for the register book. "How many nights would you like?"

Erik raised a single finger.

The clerk continued as he turned the book around, "Single room. $5.65 a day. Bathroom privileges are extra. Would you care to sign the register now, sir?"

Erik nodded and signed.

"I would like to advise you that for all those who ship out with the military, we are happy to invite you back at the rate you paid today when you return."

Erik nodded as he handed over the requested payment, and the clerk handed over the key.

The transaction completed, the clerk offered, "We have a porter available to help you with your luggage."

Erik waved his hand to refuse the service.

Once on the sixth floor, he found his room, and Ronnie's room was across the hallway, as the clerk said. As an intelligence officer, Erik knew Ronnie would keep to himself and would be suspicious if someone walked up to him and started talking to him. So, the most effective thing was to let Ronnie come to him. Erik went to Ronnie's door, juddered the handle for a few seconds, then proceeded to his door and fumbled with the key in the knob. The door behind opened suddenly, revealing Ronnie Schan.

"Excuse me. Did you see someone just trying to get in here?" Ronnie asked with a disgusted look.

Erik pointed down the hallway as he explained. "Yes. Some kids ran that way." Moments like those were always tense, and Erik knew his timing had to be perfect as he made his pitch. "Ronnie Schan, is that you?" Erik tilted his head and gave an inquisitive look. Ronnie looked at Erik, trying to recall his face or a place where they could have met or his name.

"I thought I recognized you." Erik extended his hand. "How have you been?" Erik also knew this part was all about making individuals comfortable, convincing them you were not a threat, and making them feel important. "We worked in the same department. I saw you from a distance. I'm Erik."

Ronnie extended his hand to meet Erik's. "Erik?" Ronnie replied. He was not yet done studying him. "What department was that?"

Erik mumbled under his breath, "I'm a squirrel," Ronnie squinted his eyes as he retracted his hand as Erik continued. "Just like you." Erik showed Ronnie the intelligence bullion badge on his left arm and then pointed to Ronnie's left arm.

"Small world," Ronnie replied.

"Indeed." Erik nodded to Ronnie and suggested that he come with him while he dropped off his bags and got some food. It worked.

Erik placed his luggage in his room. Ronnie felt comfortable and struck up a conversation. "Where do you want to go?"

"I am up for anything." Erik grabbed the three bottles of VIS-INE eye drops and placed them in his pocket. "I just got back from across the pond about a week ago."

"What is the weather like there?"

"Cold and wet." Erik emerged into the hallway and locked his door. "Another thing," Erik said, just above a whisper. "The food is very bland. You need to use a lot of salt." After Ronnie locked his door, they proceeded to the entrance. "I'm really looking forward to American food."

"Have you heard of Longchamps?" Ronnie asked.

Erik shook his head.

"They have the best seafood."

Erik mouthed, "*Oh yeah.*"

Once outside, they hailed a cab and headed to Longchamps on the corner of East 42nd Street and Lexington. The taxi stopped in front of the Chanin Building, where Longchamps was located. Upon stepping out, Erik took in the Art déco architecture with buff brick, limestone, terracotta, bronze, marble, and custom-designed, colored glass ornaments.

"Have you ever been here?" Erik shook his head as he looked at the base of the building that bore black Belgian marble around the storefront windows that advertised items and the latest fashion. Longchamps took up the entire length of 42nd Street, with the lights illuminating the bustling activity inside. Directly above him were polished bronze sculptures depicting scenes of evolution, ranging from simple organisms to complex animals and plants.

Inside, a host greeted them, and they were quickly seated at a corner table, which Erik requested. Erik admired the décor, a feast for his eyes, of the nearly a dozen murals that encompassed the room. They reflected the gayest and most wicked periods in French history, dealing with the life of Louis the fifteenth before the French Revolution, when the courts were at their best and worst. The artist enhanced each mural with bright red and gold paint with a hint of gray, which represented floor tiles.

Erik took a seat against the wall as he quickly surveyed the restaurant and the people in it, locating the exits and the location of the kitchen. A young lady, the server, asked what they would like to drink, and Erik suggested two glasses of iced tea each because they were both parched. Ronnie agreed. Erik gestured to Ronnie to take the salt shaker as he reminded him that English food was bland. They both chuckled. Erik raised his glass and made a toast to the defeat of the Nazis as Ronnie nodded in agreement. At that moment, the server took their orders, and Ronnie excused himself to the restroom.

Erik recalled when he was in training, an operative's job didn't always involve turning people into assets but gaining their trust. In return, they would betray their country. However, in cases like his, Ronnie was meant to end. Often, the solution to a problem was that simple. Erik knew killing Ronnie was necessary. In the end, he lacked regard for Ronnie's life, remorse, or empathy, which made him effective at what he does. Erik opened two bottles of VISINE eye drops and dispensed one with each glass of Ronnie's iced tea. Moments later, Ronnie came back.

The server brought their dinners. Erik had the sizzling hamburger steak platter with fried onions, mushrooms sauté, raw spinach, and mashed potatoes. Ronnie had ordered sizzling sirloin steak, sliced mushrooms, sautéed string beans, a whole baked tomato, and Longchamps potatoes. Ronnie took a bite of his sirloin, and the pleasure impregnated all his senses. He savored several bites, then took a gulp of his tea. Erik could see he was reminiscing as their eyes met.

"Reminds me of home," Ronnie mumbled as he took another bite. "My mom's cooking."

Erik smiled back. With each task, Erik learns a lot about himself. This was the first time he betrayed someone to serve a higher cause.

"Are you married?" Ronnie asked.

Erik nodded as he enjoyed his meal.

"Any kids?"

Erik nodded again. "They're in Virginia." Erik gathered his thoughts. "I hope I can get some sleep tonight."

Ronnie placed his glass down after taking a sip. "A lot on your mind?"

Erik nodded.

"Why don't you try to take some deep breaths and slowly exhale? It will help you get there before sack time." Erik raised an eyebrow in a questioning glance as Ronnie chuckled. "I know. It sounds crazy." Ronnie raised his hand so he could finish.

Erik gestured for him to continue. "Trust me. I've been doing it ever since the war started."

"What time are you being picked up?" Erik inquired.

"Zero six hundred. You?"

"Same." Erik leaned forward. "Once we get to England, it will just be the beginning. If we work hard, we're going to win this war maybe in a year or two."

"You think so?" Ronnie replied as he leaned back.

Erik's eyes seemed to drift to some inner place, his passion surging as he explained, "The Germans have been kicking other people's asses since 1939." He took a swallow of his drink. "I guess it's time to show Hitler we are going to kick his ass."

Ronnie nodded in agreement.

"Tens of thousands of guys like you and I will return to wherever we came from in this great country of ours. We will hide things we saw from others because we do not wish to remember the horrors we experienced. When we get back, I hope people will know the sacrifices we made, no matter what we did during the war."

Erik paused in thought and closed his eyes for a moment. When he opened his eyes, they were tense and focused. "However, the politicians will thank us and say they care. I hope they care about those lives dramatically touched by the war."

Ronnie stared into Erik's eyes, which were blazing. He recalled the horrors he had seen before and the mourning of his friends.

Ronnie looked at Erik deeper in his eyes, analyzing him, and was in awe of his intensity. Erik looked away, not wanting Ronnie to look into parts of his mind that are the darkest pits of hell where no light shines, nor would anyone want to explore.

Suddenly, Ronnie felt a splitting sensation through his eyes and temples. Pain extended toward the back of his head. The server came with the tabs, and Erik gave the server a ten-dollar bill and advised her to keep the change. He made his way to the other side of the table to assist Ronnie. Erik walked by Ronnie's side, who was stumbling. Erik's eyes met Ronnie's. The man's expression was as if someone grabbed a hot rod and pressed it against one side of his head. Pain pulsed with every heartbeat, mixed with intense nausea and dizziness.

Once on the street, Erik hailed a cab and had them drive to the hotel. Cabs are comfortable at first because you are off your feet, but the big iron springs under the seat make it very stiff. With the sudden lunges forward and sudden stops, the cab moved along steadily, but that made Ronnie feel worse. It didn't help that the cab was dirty from all the individuals that came before, and it smelled. Erik did his best to comfort Ronnie, even though he knew he was dying. Situations like that, seeing an innocent person dying in his arms, demanded he be detached from his feelings. In the end, Erik broke Ronnie's trust.

Once they reached the Iroquois, Erik shielded his and Ronnie's faces as they walked through the lobby. Nearing Ronnie's room, Erik pulled out the key. Once the door was unlocked, he asked Ronnie to help open the door with what strength he had. He gently placed Ronnie in bed and made the dying man as comfortable as he could. Erik checked Ronnie's pulse on his wrist, and the blood was flowing as if it were gas being pumped by a fuel injector. Things were kicking in with an elevated heartbeat, unintentionally trembling, and dilated pupils.

"Erik, what's happening to me?" Ronnie mumbled as Erik tried to ease his pain. "I'm scared." Ronnie squeezed Erik's hand, and fear filled Ronnie's eyes. Ronnie's trembling intensified as the tetrahydrozoline took effect, and his breaths slowly became shorter and shorter as the minutes passed. An hour went by. Ronnie's head rolled on the pillow, releasing the last breath from his lungs.

Using a handkerchief, Erik picked up the phone, ordered room service, and waited. Once the food came, he advised the attendant to leave it in the hallway and waited till he thought the coast was clear before opening the door. He searched for a storage closet to hide the body, casually walking up and down the hallway. Erik knew he had prepared for every aspect of the mission, like hiding a body, not getting caught, and not being charged with murder. Of course, being able to do it and planning it are different things.

At the far end of the hallway, by the stairs, there was a storage closet, which was locked. Erik studied the lock. It was a standard room door lock. He headed back to the room, got two paper clips, and folded one in half, bending one end at a ninety-degree angle to make a handle to form a tension wrench. For the second one, he opened one side of the paperclip, extended one bar, and twisted it up and down to make a rake pick. After that, he stripped Ronnie to his undergarments and secured him under the room service cart with the tablecloth concealing him. He tested the cart, and it could move easily.

He then gathered all of Ronnie's belongings and packed them into his suitcase. Lucky for Erik, air conditioning in hotels was not the norm in those days and the windows could open. He opened the window with a cloth over his fingertips, leaving no trace of himself. After checking to see if there was any activity in the alleyway, he tossed Ronnie's suitcase out of the window. Erik stood and waited for any additional activity. Moments later, a man emerged from the darkness and slowly made his way to the suitcase, like a rodent curious about a strange object in their environment. He made sure no one was looking, then disappeared into the darkness with his prize.

Erik opened the door, took a quick glance up and down the hallway, rolled the cart out, placed the do not disturb placard over the knob, locked the door, then headed to the supply closet. Once at the closet, Erik inserted the tension wrench in the lower part of the keyhole and the rake in the upper part. He pushed against the tension wrench and moved the rake back and forth. Within a minute, Erik unlocked the door and placed the room service cart inside. Lastly, Erik inserted Ronnie's room key into the closet's knob and broke it off in the keyhole.

Once inside his own hotel room, Erik called the front desk and requested a wake-up call at five-thirty and went to bed. This might be the only night he would get a good night's rest. He lay on his bed, staring at the ceiling in the darkness. Even with the blinds down, street lamps penetrated into the room. Traffic still rumbled outside, not as bad during the day, but Erik still heard it. He remembered everything Ronnie said, took a deep breath, and slowly exhaled. He did that several times and thought, *I'm okay. I'm all right*.

He was almost on the way to England. He reminded himself not to forget his passes when he would surely be approached. Despite his best efforts, he couldn't keep the gloomy thoughts away, lying there in 1944, knowing Jamie and the boys were buried in 1961. Ironically, in two months, his other self would appear in France trying to save Rommel. Erik hit his forehead several times as he thought, *Stop thinking so much of what happened. And stop thinking as if Jamie is upstairs at the Kennedy Warren putting the boys to bed.*

Erik wished he could change his own history, but he couldn't change history for his own benefit. He could make things worse if he saved Jamie and the boys that dreadful day. Sure, he would be in a much happier place. Erik wondered how that would have been. *Cut it out, cut it out, cut it out*, he told himself.

Erik tried to focus on all the things he would have to do in the coming days. Erik had to get ready for whatever lay ahead, but he didn't know what that was. The only thing Erik knew was he was stranded in obscurity.

CHAPTER 13

NO WAY BACK; JUST THROUGH

"Without heroes, we are all plain people and don't know how far we can go."
— Bernard Malamud

NEW YORK CITY, NEW YORK, MAY 28, 1944

Erik walked into the lobby to find an army lieutenant standing in front of the entrance. The emotionless officer was waiting to greet him and take him to the airport. As Erik drew closer, the man approached him with a cold and stoic expression. Once they were within three feet of one another, they exchanged words.

"Sir, do you have everything you need?" the lieutenant asked.

"I happened to forget my umbrella."

"Sir, we will provide one for you."

The lieutenant did an about-face, and Erik followed him out. Outside was a black 1939 Lincoln K Series limousine and an olive drab 1942 Ford staff car sedan bearing government plates parked by the curb. The lieutenant offered to take his bag as he motioned to Erik that he would ride in the black limousine. There was a non-uniformed driver and passenger inside the car and the indistinct figure of a man watching from the back seat.

Erik quickly analyzed the man through the misted window,

which made the facial details impossible to distinguish. He wore pince-nez-framed spectacles with rounded lenses and held what appeared to be a cigarette holder with a cigarette end glowing bright orange. He also had neatly trimmed hair under a fedora, a rectangular head with a strong thrusting jaw, and what appeared to be cigarette holders with cigarette ends glowing bright orange. Once Erik started walking toward the car, the passenger got out and stood in front of the car. The agent reached across to open the door that led to the back seat. Erik climbed in, and the man shut the door firmly.

"Welcome, major." A deep, commanding voice welcomed Erik as he slowly turned his head, recognizing the person next to him was FDR. "We have a lot to talk about." Erik knew that there was no practice or planning to simulate situations like that. "First, it's not every day you betray a fellow service member and kill them to serve the greater good of the free world." Roosevelt paused for a moment. "We need to remove the body. Where is it?"

Erik nodded. "Sixth floor, maintenance closet at the end of the hallway by the stairs."

Roosevelt motioned to the man in the front passenger seat to take care of it. Once he exited the car, it lunged forward and headed toward LaGuardia. "I need you to be frank with me. Is that clear?" Roosevelt tilted his head down toward Erik, squinting his eyes. Erik felt a rush of adrenaline through his veins as he adjusted to the conversation on the fly. "Were you at Kellogg's Diner in August of 1940?"

Erik hated the feeling that he knew nothing about where the conversation was heading. Roosevelt removed his cigarette holder from his lips, tilted his head back to look down his nose at Erik through the pince-nez, seeming like a hawk before a kill. "I have no time for bullshit. Were you there?"

Roosevelt was caught up in something he didn't understand.

Erik felt FDR already knew the answer to his question, so the best thing to do was to tell the truth. "Yes, I was, Mr. President."

As Roosevelt placed his cigarette holder in his mouth, he gave a casual smirk and nodded. "When you left, you didn't recognize me sitting in the back." He gestured to the empty front passenger seat. "Grayson passed you by and overheard you talking to Mr. Scherff, Nikola Tesla's assistant." He took a long draw on his cigarette, then glared at Erik through the smoke. "Grayson overheard you two talking about Time travel. And that you have done it before." He glanced at Erik with a rather intense inquiry. "Don't worry, I will tell nobody about you. Erik, I know everything about you."

Erik merely stared, unprepared for such an eventuality.

Roosevelt waved a dismissive hand. "I know about the work you have done with the government. Excellent work, I would say. Prevented the Nazis from getting the atomic bomb. Single-handedly defeated the Nazis in the air war over Britain in 1940. Also, you have a star on the wall at CIA headquarters in Langley." Roosevelt shook his head. "I'll admit, I don't understand all of it. However, as the President of the United States, knowledge is not an issue. Acting on that knowledge is the mission I want you to do."

Roosevelt sat quietly and fixed his eyes on Erik as he puffed his cigarette. "So, Erik, how many times have you traveled through time?"

Erik answered, his monotone voice was firm and without emotion, "Four, including this time."

Roosevelt's face took on a stern and amazed look.

"I have taken on many roles. They placed me at pivotal junctures during this war because someone altered it in its course."

Roosevelt had a look of astonishment as he removed his cigarette. "Like an actor."

Erik nodded. "I have to respond to the challenge of preserving history."

The Ford and Lincoln were on a road within LaGuardia Airport leading to the aircraft that would take Erik to England. The sun rose from the horizon and its rays breached through the fog that lingered above asphalt runways that stretched like a spider's web. The cars neared a sleek, shiny aluminum aircraft which could be compared to an elongated fish. Some would say it looked like a whale with smooth curves. It had a circular cross-section, a snub nose, and a triple-fined tail. On each wing was a pair of low-mounted, two-row 18-cylinder air-cooled radial engines.

Roosevelt pointed to the Lockheed Constellation, indicating it was the aircraft Erik would be taking. Erik nodded, familiar with the model since he flew in one in 1948 with Howard Hughes. Behind the Plexiglas windows in the cockpit, the crew inside stared idly at the cars, in particular the black Lincoln limousine, as they approached. Once within walking distance of the aircraft, the cars stopped. The officer from the Ford stepped out and grabbed Erik's bag, handing it over to a member of the crew. As the crew member headed back to the aircraft, the staff car left.

"Mr. President, we are here."

"Thank you, George." At that moment, George stepped out of the car and assumed his position outside the car. Roosevelt handed over a sealed envelope. "I have written a letter to General Eisenhower. Would you deliver it for me?"

Erik nodded.

"Good. Also, Eisenhower should open the letter as soon as you hand it to him. I would like you to know the contents of the letter." Erik tried to protest, but Roosevelt dismissed the subject with a short sideways jerk of his cigarette, then gave it a last draw and killed it in the ashtray.

"I'm placing you under Major General Henry JF Miller as his

intelligence officer." Erik absorbed the details as Roosevelt hand-ed another envelope to him. "This is your cover story. You will repeat it to General Miller if he asks you about your background. If he investigates that story," Roosevelt paused to point to the envelope, "you have nothing to worry about. Once you have it memorized, destroy it."

"Thank you, Mr. President."

"Erik, once you are in London, you will stay at Claridge's. When you arrive at the airport, you will be driven to a build-ing named The Royal Historic Conservatory, which is at 3 Mat-thew Parker Street. The code word is proteus, and your number is seventeen." Erik nodded, making mental notes. "I'm advising Eisenhower that what you say goes." Erik nodded. "I've never seen a more impressive display of loyalty and service to our country." Roosevelt extended his hand to thank Erik.

"You are welcome, Mr. President."

Roosevelt got Erik's attention one last time. "Erik, I need every advantage to win this war. You can make that happen right now because you know the future and those damn Nazis don't."

"Mr. President, believe me, the information I know is more powerful than any weapon. When others find out what I know, it's enough reason for them to try to kill me."

Roosevelt left Erik with this thought. "I know what you do isn't easy, but I know it's important that you are aware your life could save tens of thousands of lives."

Once on board the plane, Erik took his seat, as did the steward-ess. Moments later, the engines came to life one at a time, billowing black smoke, a thunderous roar reverberating throughout the plane, and the sputtering propellers slowly moved in perfect harmony with each other. Approximately twenty minutes later, they were at their cruising altitude. The stewardess started making Erik break-fast, and the pilot introduced himself. Erik was kind, but distant.

Like every other time Erik went back in time, there could be one or several other individuals who were also there from the future to change the past. Finding, confronting, and taking down such an elaborate, covert network was the ultimate challenge because they knew there were individuals like Erik there to put history back to how it was supposed to be.

When Erik was a part of the O.G.D.S. Team 42, he had a whole team helping him. However, whenever he went back, he worked alone and had to rely on everything he learned at the farm and utilize any resources he might find on the way. Another disadvantage of trying to find Erik's adversary was there was no solid intelligence that could point him in the right direction. The individual or individuals would be hiding in plain sight, just like Erik, with all the same training and skills.

On the other side, Erik might have to impersonate Albert Van Loop if he was unsuccessful in finding the mole within the allied headquarters. His situation was like a gigantic labyrinth with a jigsaw puzzle of information that has to be analyzed in the field, and if he was not careful, he could end up being killed. It was not like he was a detective where each piece of the puzzle he found led to his enemy. However, if his enemy knew they were going to be compromised, they would strike first—like with his encounter with the Mossad operative.

If Erik had any luck, they would confront each other at the same time, but only one of them would walk away from that. Erik also had to consider he could be up against an entire network of temporal operatives. Either way, he would need to keep fighting to correct history for the better. Until that time, the unknown operatives and Erik were looking for each other, and when they found each other, they would give Erik the answers he was looking for. Notably: Why would they change the past?

Erik asked the stewardess for a pen and a sheet of paper. Once he got them, he wrote Jamie a letter. Although she and the boys had died, writing letters to her made Erik feel that she was still alive.

Dearest Jamie,

Our forces continue to grow. As long as we keep our spirits up and remain focused, once we unleash our forces on mainland Europe, we will push the Germans back and end this war. I long to see you and hold you in my arms and speak to you. My duties keep me busy, but I hope that the powers that be will allow you to be near me. Until then, I will remain most affectionately yours with love in my heart.

Your loving husband,
Erik

After that, Erik leaned his chair back and tried to get some rest.

CHAPTER 14

THE INTRICATE BEGINNING

"You'd be astounded by the things I know."

— Elijah, *The Originals*

LONDON, ENGLAND, MAY 29, 1944

The weather was mild, with layers of cumulus clouds in various shades of gray covering the sun. Once the aircraft landed and taxied to its assigned location, Erik got up and exited. An Army lieutenant was waiting for him with an olive-drab Ford sedan bearing government plates parked fifty yards away from the aircraft, with a uniformed driver. The indistinct lieutenant greeted Erik with a salute and offered to take his luggage. Erik noticed a white circle was added around the star on the Ford. To prepare for the invasion of Normandy, the lieutenant advised they painted all vehicles with white circles. It was regulation for all military-issued vehicles in the European Theater.

Erik was driven to 3 Matthew Parker Street. As they headed deeper into London, Erik noticed strategically placed barrage balloons up and down the Thames River. The balloons defended ground targets against Luftwaffe attacks, making their approach more difficult. They were held by cables secured to pulleys on trucks, transitioning from shades of blue into a shining silver as the sun repositioned itself in the sky.

Erik focused on his surroundings. On both sides of the narrow, cobbled streets were weathered brick houses that appeared to be at least a century old, of three and four stories, with shops at ground level and the owner's residence above. Individuals strolled on the sidewalks engaged in conversation or keeping to themselves while they looked inside the store windows. Some people could be the shop owners, who sat or stood at the entrances.

Groups of young people hung around the street corners. The Blitz was over, but there were men in white denim pullover shirts that were soiled with dirt and sweat working on the roads. The people in London didn't know what Erik did, that there was going to be a new threat that would terrify the city—V rockets.

Eventually, the car came to a halt, and the lieutenant stepped around it and opened the door for Erik.

Before them stood a weathered, two-story brick building with blacked-out windows because of air raids. It was nestled perfectly with the surrounding buildings of the quiet neighborhood. The residents hardly paid any attention to the building, even though they passed it each day. They didn't have time to notice the gold ornate lettering of the sign which read, *The Royal Historic Conservatory*. In fact, they probably wouldn't even notice the sign if they tried.

Erik passed through the black cast-iron gate that surrounded the courtyard in front, and a sentry at the entrance asked for his ID before he continued, but something caught his eye. There was a man wearing a charcoal suit with a hard enamel lapel pin. This had a black background and the polished gold outline of an alligator's head emerging from the water with its mouth open. Within its mouth, peach in color, was a Venus fly trap, also outlined in polished gold, open reaching for a fly. The pin mesmerized Erik with its deadly beauty. The man nodded at Erik with a haughty expression, then walked down the sidewalk.

Inside, the Royal Historic Conservatory's extreme cleanliness was immediately apparent. Everything was immaculate, from the vacuumed carpets to the dust-free furnishings. Fifteen feet from the entrance was a desk with a man behind it who kept a keen eye on who was coming and going. He was the gatekeeper. There appeared to be no papers on or around the gatekeeper's desk, including the drawers, except for one page in front of him. The only other object on the desk was a phone.

However, there were some things not visible to the naked eye. The desk had a steel-reinforced front, in case attackers forced their way in. In addition, there was a button under the lip of the desk, within arm's reach, which could be pressed in case of trouble or if additional security was needed. Finally, on the gatekeeper's hip was an Enfield No.2 Mk I, the British standard revolver during World War II. To those passing by, the building was The Royal Historic Conservatory. However, for those who were granted access behind the gatekeeper, the Royal Historic Conservatory dissolved into a branch office of the Supreme Headquarters Allied Expeditionary Force.

The gatekeeper, a staff sergeant, welcomed Erik. "Good evening, Major. How can I help you?"

He handed his ID over. "I'm Major Erik Foge, reporting to Major General Henry JF Miller." The staff sergeant motioned for Erik to take a seat. At that moment, the phone broke the silence in the lobby. The staff sergeant picked up the receiver. A tense look came over his face as he glanced at Erik slowly, his eyes haunted by some inner anxiety. "Yes, sir." He nodded. "Okay, sir." Yes, sir." He hung up. "The general will be out shortly."

A few minutes passed, and the door opened to reveal a white-haired, fair-skinned gentleman who held the rank of Major

General. As he approached, Erik stood up, snapped to attention, and saluted the senior officer. Erik felt the general was personable from his warm grin as he returned the salute and extended his hand to welcome Erik. "Welcome, Major Foojay?" He stumbled over the last name.

Erik assisted him.

"Foogee? Is that French?"

Erik shook his head and explained that after the First World War, his family came to America, but it wasn't a good time to be a German. They changed the spelling to make it sound American.

Miller nodded and rubbed his chin as he stared at Erik. "Do you like Greek mythology?"

"I adore it."

Miller rubbed his chin. "Who is your favorite god?"

Erik smirked and replied with the utmost confidence. "Proteus."

Miller looked for an explanation.

"He knew all things—past, present, and future—but disliked divulging what he knew."

Miller smiled and gestured to Erik to follow him as he approached the desk. "Sergeant, this is Major Erik Foge. He is my intelligence officer. Remember his name and face." The sergeant nodded. "We need to assign him a number."

"Sir, I would prefer the number seventeen." Erik interrupted.

"Sergeant, give the major the number seventeen."

"Yes, sir." The staff sergeant grabbed the number off the board directly behind him and gave it to the general.

Handing the number over to Erik, Miller pointed to his left pocket in which the number was to be placed. Once that was done, they entered another room full of commotion, with teams updating information on German troop movements on and around the Normandy coast. As they approached Miller's office, the general asked, "So, is seventeen your lucky number or your jersey number from when you played sports?"

"No, sir. In the Bible, the number seventeen symbolizes overcoming the enemy."

Miller clapped his hands together to indicate they needed to get down to business. "As you already know, I'm Major General Henry JF Miller. I am the commander of the Ninth Army Air Force Service Command." He leaned back in his chair, picking up a letter that was open on his desk and perusing it as he asked, "Who am I working with? Tell me about your background."

Erik answered with the cover story the president had presented him with. "I attended the Virginia Military Institute and received my bachelor's degree in military history. Since I love the Napoleonic Wars, I traveled to Europe and Russia during summer breaks prior to World War One. I am fluent in German and Russian. When America went to war against Germany in 1917, I enlisted as a commissioned officer. During boot camp, Major Dennis E. Nolan, the Chief Intelligence Officer for the American Expeditionary Forces, approached me and asked me to work for the Military Information Division, G2, because of my language skills.

"I can draw on the full range of intelligence fields—human, photographic, and signals—for operational intelligence, as well as political and economic intelligence. I was one of the people who found out about the separate peace treaty between the new Bolshevik government of Russia and the Central Powers. After the war, they reduced the Military Information Division in size, and I became a history teacher.

"In 1942, the OSS recruited me with the rank of a major. I've been working as an analyst in Washington since then, and now I'm here."

"I must say, that is astonishing." Miller set down the letter. Erik saw from a glance it was from Eisenhower and introduced Erik as an intelligence officer. "Normally, I would have an individual's service record before I meet them." Miller leaned forward and glared at Erik. "So, where is your service record? I asked General Eisenhower about it, and he told me not to worry about it." He crossed his arms against his chest. "I cannot question my superior officer, but that doesn't mean I can't question you. So, I will ask again, where is your service record?"

Erik replied in a cold, calculated tone. "Sir, a conflict between us would not end well."

"For you or me?"

Erik said nothing.

"It is my intention to speak to General Eisenhower about this tomorrow. If you are planning to be working for me, you will provide me with new information so we can cripple the Nazis and prepare for the assault on Normandy. Is that understood, major?"

"Yes, sir."

"I expect more from your credentials. Is that understood?"

"Yes, sir."

"We are going to be busy right until the invasion." He looked at his watch. "Major, you need to be here by oh-seven-hundred hours tomorrow."

Erik saluted Miller, studying the general. Even though he graduated from West Point, Miller wasn't a born leader. He would push that weight on others who didn't attend, and even though Erik was in uniform, his past intimidated the general. Erik knew Miller was smart as a whip and knew he could do his job better than any one of his peers. However, his sense of humor was limited to only those who held his rank or above.

"You are dismissed."

Erik saluted again, did an about-face, and left. Once in the lobby of The Royal Historic Conservatory, the sergeant asked for the number back and called for a car for Erik. He thanked the sergeant and exited the building. He paused at a curb and looked at his surroundings, which were not much different from when he was there in November of 1944 with Jamie, before they headed to the United States. While buildings across London prepared for the greatest invasion ever seen, Erik found it amazing how the people of the city went about their daily business knowing there was a war raging just across the channel.

Despite that, nothing seemed out of the ordinary. The buildings softened the shunting trains from Wetherspoons, ringing and rumbling, becoming melodic as they traveled further. It all seemed so safe and tranquil, but that would soon change because the V1 rockets would start hitting London in the next couple of weeks.

A car pulled up for Erik. He climbed in and they headed to Claridge's, where he checked in, destroyed the cover letter, and got a bite to eat before calling it a night.

CHAPTER 15

THESE COMBINATIONS HAVE NOT BEEN BEFORE

"Just once, I'd like something to go as planned, ya know?"

— Andy Weir, *The Martian*

LONDON, ENGLAND

It was a crisp, cloudless day, with a slight breeze sweeping down the bustling streets and open areas. The sun's warmth made it a wonderful day. Erik had been walking for hours. It seemed odd that the traffic was light on the streets and sidewalks, as if a curfew were in place. But that didn't surprise him because it was wartime. Eventually, he took the eastern approach, walking through the New Palace Yard, a large grounds northwest of the Palace of Westminster. While Big Ben was in front of him, the most prominent tower in London, he felt intolerably lonely.

Suddenly, Erik heard someone calling his name, but no one was around. He kept walking and looking. He heard his name again, this time closer. He stopped and looked around, then felt a warm presence. As he turned his head, the blood drained from his face, and he was left speechless by the sensation. Jamie stood there, as beautiful as the last time he saw her on that dreadful morning. Joy exploded on Erik's face. He ran to her and stopped inches from her.

"Jamie… is it you?" he asked, and she nodded. "What happened? Where are the boys?"

"They're safe. You will be great today. He is waiting for you. You must wake up."

"I don't want to. I want to stay with you. I need you so much! I love you!"

"I am with you, and I will always love you, but you must wake up. He is waiting for you."

MAY 30, 1944

The phone rang through the silence of the room and penetrated Erik's ears. He fought like a fish caught in a net to remove the sheet and blanket and get to the phone. He picked up the receiver, and the pleasant voice on the other end advised him it was his wake-up call. After placing the receiver down, he turned on the lamp and grabbed the photo of Jamie and Big Ben from 1944. He took a deep breath and whispered, "I wish I knew who *he* is that's waiting for me."

Erik had an hour to get ready and eat breakfast before the car would pick him up. He did his morning routines, and before heading out, he grabbed Jamie's picture and FDR's letter. Once in the hotel's restaurant, he placed his order and got lost in his thoughts. He wondered what the days ahead held for him or if the days even had him in mind. Erik closed his eyes and thought to himself, *God tells me where I'm heading. I don't know what is in store for me.*

After breakfast, he headed outside and waited for the car scheduled to pick him up. A few minutes later, it appeared and took him back to the Royal Historic Conservatory. The guard outside welcomed Erik. Inside the lobby, the same sergeant from the day before greeted him with a friendly tone.

"Good morning, Major Foge."

"Morning, sergeant." The sergeant handed Erik his number and buzzed him in.

The moment Erik entered, he had to show his number to the armed sentry, then was immersed into a world of calculating and analyzing troop movements, deciphering German messages, organizing allied troops, arranging logistics, and every component of an enormous amphibious landing such as Operation Overlord. Standing in front of him was a young lieutenant dressed in a sharp uniform.

"Sir, General Miller wants you to visit him in his office before you start your day."

Erik followed. He knew General Miller insisted on controlling every aspect of his operation, including the people that worked under him. Erik didn't realize if Miller had the power to ask for his military record. He knew, however, he would face questions about his cover story in time, and people would start testing him, and he would have no choice but to use his connection to FDR. In the meantime, he had to grit his teeth and roll the dice. The lieutenant knocked at the door designated for Major General Henry JF Miller.

"Come in." A deep voice ordered.

Miller looked up and addressed the lieutenant. "Dismissed." When the junior officer was gone, Erik entered the office and closed the door behind him.

"Erik, sit, please. I'd like to have a word with you before you start your day."

Erik sat quietly. He knew it was wise to answer the questions directly, and it was a matter of figuring out what Miller knew or didn't know. So, he mentally crossed his fingers and hoped to get out of Miller's office as quickly as he could.

"General Eisenhower and I go way back. We went to West Point together, and we were commissioned together. With your background and time in service, you could have been a general by now. However, it's not my fault that you quit and came back." Miller stood up and peered down at Erik. "Will that be a source of tension or embarrassment for you?"

"No, Sir."

"Good, because I don't give a shit. We're in the business of defeating the Nazis, major."

A knock came at the door. "Come in!"

"General Eisenhower's office just called. He can see you now in the library, sir."

"I'll be talking to you later," Miller addressed Erik with a bitter tone.

"General Eisenhower is requesting the major to come too."

"Thank you." Miller walked around his desk as Erik stood at attention and made way for Miller to go ahead of him. Miller glared at Erik. The expression on the general's face indicated he was slightly confused, yet hiding his irritation. "Follow along, Major; we cannot keep General Eisenhower waiting."

Miller and Erik headed to the library in silence. Erik noticed fewer people in those areas; however, the armed military police presence had increased. As they walked along, they eventually reached a solid, oak-stained double door with five guards, one of whom acted as the point man who was attentive to what was happening around them. The point man had a clipboard with a list of permitted individuals and the number on the badge associated with that individual. After that brief security check, they allowed Miller and Erik in.

They entered a large, comfortable room with a center table

covered by a green baize cloth. On top of the cloth was a detailed topographic map of the Normandy beaches and surrounding areas. It showed the physical features, elevation differences, and landscape changes. The map also included roads, highways, railways, and civilian and military structures. Around the library were a dozen easy chairs and two sofas with end tables on either side. Neatly carved, dark oak bookcases lined three of the walls.

Because of the air raids during the Blitz, most of the books were placed in the basement, and the shelves remained bare. In addition, thick, heavy, double-blackout curtains hung over the windows, again because of the air raids, muffling the drumming rain and roaring wind outside.

Twelve senior officers talked quietly amongst each other in small groups. At the head of the table was Eisenhower's chief of staff, Major General Walter Bedell Smith, conversing with Deputy Supreme Commander Air Chief Marshal Tedder. In addition, the naval commander, Admiral Ramsay, stood close by, along with Air Chief Marshal Leigh-Mallory and General Smith, who was the only officer dressed informally. Erik noticed there was no Field Marshal Montgomery, who would be in charge of the D-Day assault. *Thank God*, he thought to himself. General Bradly was also absent.

A decisive conference had been called at the last minute. That would begin at seven thirty. The most significant thing that would be brought up was the weather. Everyone would hear the latest forecasts from the meteorologists. The doors swung open at seven twenty-five. The three senior meteorologists, led by their chief, Group Captain JN Stagg of the Royal Air Force, strolled into the room and had a casual chat. They moved to the head of the table and stood by General Smith. All that remained was for Eisenhower to arrive.

At exactly seven thirty, seeming like it was orchestrated, the door opened, and Eisenhower appeared. It was like seeing a picture from Time Life Magazine. Eisenhower was neat in his dark-green battle dress. While he made his way around the room, he greeted his old friends with the faintest flicker of a smile. However, a mask of worry and stress showed through the smile as he discussed all the details of Operation Overlord. Everybody knew the seriousness of the invasion and that the different components had to fall into place perfectly to pull it off. Eventually, Eisenhower made his way toward Erik, staring at him with an enigmatic expression, with one eyebrow in a questioning slant. Then Eisenhower glanced at Miller, and his face warmed with a slight grin. "Hank, good to see you again."

"Good morning, sir."

Again, Eisenhower made eye contact with Erik as he lowered his head and prepared what he was going to say next. "The president spoke highly of you, Major." Eisenhower extended his hand toward Erik. "How do you pronounce your name?"

"Foge, it has a long E, sir." Erik reached into his pocket and handed over the envelope from FDR to Eisenhower. "Sir, the president ordered me to give this to you, and for you to open it immediately."

"Right now, major?"

"Sir, yes, sir."

Eisenhower stepped away and read the letter, and his breath caught in his throat. He glanced at Erik, his eyes wide with surprise.

May 28, 1944, 11 pm
The White House, Washington

Dear General Eisenhower, Supreme Headquarters Allied Expeditionary Force,

It's with great pleasure I write you this letter regarding Major Erik Foge. You must keep what I am going to tell you to yourself and not disclose it to any member of your staff at the Supreme Headquarters of the Allied Expeditionary Force. As you are aware, Prime Minister Churchill and I have communicated and agreed that if Major Foge needs to make any modifications to Operation Overlord, you will make the necessary adjustments. There may be questions in your mind regarding my intentions; however, I am confident that he knows, in great detail, what to expect from the German military and their staff in the days to come, including Hitler himself. Although your staff and others may request an explanation, you should remain firmly in support of what Major Foge says.

As I have mentioned previously, you have the support of myself and Prime Minister Churchill. As a result of the Russian offensive on the Eastern Front, more Germans are being killed, and a larger quantity of equipment is being destroyed than by England and the United States combined. If Operation Overload is a complete success, it is the beginning of many big objectives that will be in store for our countries in order to defeat the German military and the Third Reich.

It is imperative that you destroy this letter as soon as you have read it to ensure the security of this information. The Germans should not be aware of our plans or the major.

Best of luck, General.
FDR

Eisenhower motioned to Erik to follow him. Once they were away from the others, Eisenhower asked in just above a whisper, "With your modifications, how sure are you that Overlord will be successful?"

"Sir, if the Germans still believe that the invasion will come at Pas de Calais, I would say we will have an advantage." Eisenhower nodded in silence. "However, if I may put it politely, sir, if I am not given complete and autonomous control of this situation to make adjustments, the landings in Normandy could be disastrous." Eisenhower nodded again. "Sir, where are General Bradley and Field Marshal Montgomery?"

"General Bradley is on holiday in Scotland till tomorrow, and Field Marshal Montgomery is with Prime Minister Churchill. He is being advised there are going to be some changes, and he will have to accept them." He gestured to Captain Stagg. "I will introduce you after he gives his weather report."

"Thank you, sir."

Eisenhower walked to the front of the room and gestured to Captain Stagg, giving him the floor. Stagg walked to the center and began his briefing after clearing his throat. "Gentlemen, there have been some rapid and unexpected developments in the situation." Every eye in the room, every anxious face, was focused on him, including Eisenhower, who was eager to know if there was a slender ray of hope.

He took a deep breath and slowly exhaled to calm his nerves. He continued, "A new weather front had been spotted, which will move up the English Channel and gradually clear the assault areas of Normandy. This clearing may last up to the morning of June sixth, then the weather will begin to deteriorate again."

General Miller asked, "Will the skies clear enough for the bombers to operate on the night of the fifth and throughout the morning of the sixth?"

"The winds will drop appreciably, so the bombers should be able to operate."

Eisenhower looked around the room and, seeing no more questions about the weather, dismissed Stagg and the other meteorological staff.

Eisenhower walked to the center of the room, at the head of the table, and looked everyone in the eye. "Gentleman, you know that in December of 1943, President Roosevelt appointed me to serve as the Supreme Allied Commander in the European Theater of Operations. We have one, only one, directive. We are to enter the continent of Europe and, with other allied nations, undertake operations aimed at the heart of Germany," he pounded his fist against the table to emphasize his next point, "and the destruction of her armed forces."

Eisenhower paused for a moment. "We have a lot of business to cover today. President Roosevelt and Prime Minister Churchill have informed me that the next person I'm going to introduce could make some modifications to Overlord." There were some disgruntled moans. "Gentlemen, I know we spent months planning this. This officer has complete confidence in this undertaking. Whatever modifications he makes is the final decision about what is going to happen." He was firm in his next words. "There will be no debates or discussion on this matter. Do I make myself clear?"

"Yes, sir," everyone, including Erik, replied in unison.

"You are my trusted and gifted colleagues, and brothers-in-arms. We are united in this crusade to liberate Europe, restore freedom, and make the world safe for democracy." Eisenhower stared in Erik's direction. "Without further ado, explaining how Operation Overlord will be successful, is best done by Major Erik Foge."

Erik felt all eyes upon him, including General Miller's, who tried to hide his disgusted expression as Erik walked to the front of the room. Once there, he turned to Eisenhower and thanked him, then glanced around the room. "America and the allied forces have been training for years, and now we're ready to strike." Erik paused for a moment and pointed to each section, Utah, Omaha, Gold, Sword, and Juno, on the Normandy Beaches. "I recommend that we have the British land at Gold, and we land at Omaha."

"Major, what is your reasoning behind that?"

"General, the beaches at Gold aren't really sand. They're pebble and rock. Thus, the British tank, the Churchill, would be better off there because there is a strong possibility they could get stuck in the sand because they're heavier than our Sherman tank." Erik paused for a moment for questions before continuing.

"Another reason is that we should not have the First and Fourth Division separated, because if things go for the worse, they can work together easier than going through the red tape with the English Fifth Division." Erik noticed Eisenhower nodded in agreement, with others reacting in the same way. "Finally, I believe our Second Ranger Regiment is more capable of taking Pointe du Hoc than the British Commandos."

"Major, Rangers have no cliff training. Why do you think the Rangers are better?"

"We can train them with the British commandos. I have two reasons why they're the better option. One, they're always combat-ready. Two, they're mentally as well as physically tough. I believe they're prepared to fight the Nazis and seize Pointe du Hoc. They will eliminate several 155 millimeter guns on the cliffs above the west flank of Omaha Beach."

Erik pointed at Pointe du Hoc. "These guns are mounted on massive wheels and secured to a central pivot on a concrete emplacement about forty feet in diameter. Furthermore, they have a reinforced concrete observation post which has helped direct the deadly fire at a range of approximately ten miles over the Utah and Omaha Beaches." Erik pointed over to the Utah and Omaha beaches. "At that distance, they could easily wreak havoc to prevent troop ships from coming too close to shore."

"General Eisenhower," Lieutenant General Hodges interjected, "we can provide the Rangers with two types of extension ladders that the Commandos will use on the first wave. We have 112-foot ladders, which will arrive in twenty-eight four-foot, tubular steel sections. Following the first wave, we could have two DUKW crafts carrying one-hundred-foot extension ladders. In addition, we should mount twin Lewis machine guns at the top of each ladder."

Erik nodded. "General Eisenhower, I would have landing crafts fitted with rocket launchers to fire grapnels and rope ladders up the cliffs just in case any craft don't make it, just as a precautionary measure."

"General Hodges, make sure that is taken care of," Eisenhower ordered, and Hodges confirmed it would be taken care of.

Erik directed a question to Eisenhower. "Sir, we set the invasion for the fifth of June?"

"That's correct, Major."

"Sir, I would recommend changing the invasion to the sixth." Grumbling echoed through the room. Eisenhower raised his hand to quiet and motioned Erik to continue. "Captain Stagg explained there was a new weather front that would move up the English Channel and gradual clearing over the assault areas of Normandy that could last throughout the morning of June sixth. I can assure you that Colonel Professor Walter Stobe, the Luftwaffe's chief meteorologist in Paris, has advised Field Marshal Von Rundstedt and Rommel that increasing cloudiness, high winds, and rain with a twenty- to thirty-mile-an-hour wind were blowing in the Channel.

"Thus, he believes it would seem unlikely that we could launch our attack during the next few days, and June fifth would be one of the few days when we would be able to land. If that were not the case, we would have to wait until July or September before we could launch our attack. So, because of that, I would postpone the landings until June sixth."

Erik looked around the room, pausing to stare at Eisenhower for a few seconds before continuing. "If you attack on the sixth, Rommel will not be at his headquarters. He will be with his family, celebrating his wife's birthday."

"Major, how will that help us?"

"The Germans think we are planning an invasion of Pas de Calais. Therefore, they will think the invasion at Normandy is a decoy and won't bother Rommel until a few hours after it begins, once they realize what's actually happening. When he gets word, he will demand Von Rundstedt to give him authority to move his panzers, and Von Rundstedt will say no. Besides that, Von Rundstedt will not disturb Hitler, who will be asleep. This is because the previous night, like every other night, Hitler watched feature films and newsreels in order to keep himself entertained. He sometimes watches two, even three films, mainly at his mountain residence in the Bavarian Alps."

One of the officers scoffed. "Major, how sure are you of that intel?"

Eisenhower interrupted in a commanding tone. "Major Foge actually visited the assault areas of Normandy as a German officer and has spoken to Rommel and even Hitler himself." He walked by Erik's side. "Gentlemen, I was on the phone with Prime Minister Churchill and President Roosevelt since five this morning about this officer, and I can tell you what they told me has convinced me that the changes in detailing and the other information he has presented is accurate. I will meet with each of you individually, and we will go over the changes in detail."

Eisenhower faced Erik. "Thank you for your input."

Erik nodded in appreciation.

"I'm surprised you are not a higher rank, considering how you see things from a different perspective. You know what's hardest about the planning of Overlord?"

Erik shook his head.

"It's the details. The small stuff. It's easy to gamble a million lives. What's hard is to see how that can hurt one person."

"General, I understand completely. Working in intelligence is the same."

"I'm sure it is." General Miller and another general approached them. "The gentleman on the left is someone I would like you to meet."

"Sir, you have a lunch meeting at twelve-thirty with your unfriendly friend," the general advised Eisenhower.

"Field Marshal Montgomery?" Erik asked.

Eisenhower laughed as the other two generals followed behind him. "I take it you have heard of him?"

Erik nodded.

"Major, what have you heard? You may speak freely. What we say stays with us."

"Sir, I believe Montgomery thinks the invasion will give German intelligence an idea of our plan. Once we establish beachheads, they'll be ready to defend a broad front." Erik raised his finger to emphasize his next point. "He would suggest a slashing blow, with Armor piercing their lines in Belgium, leaving the infantry to flow through the gap and consolidate gains across the low countries. He would say a dagger aimed at the heart of Berlin could end the war by Christmas."

Eisenhower shook his head in disbelief as he addressed the other general. "Beetle, does that sound like him?" Beetle nodded as Eisenhower made introductions. "Major, this is General Walter

Smith, my chief of staff." He then introduced Erik and faced General Miller. "Hank, I will find you another intelligence officer. The major's skills will be more useful in the theater of operation. I'm appointing him as a member of my staff starting tomorrow, and I will give him the theater rank of brigadier general." Eisenhower and Erik clasped hands and gave a firm, up-and-down shake. "Welcome aboard."

"Thank you, sir."

Eisenhower turned back to Miller. "Hank, why don't you take Erik to The Fumoir for dinner? My treat, since we are all working together." Then he turned to Erik. "I will have a car sent to your hotel tomorrow at 0600. Be at my headquarters at 0700." As he pointed at Erik, he appeared to have another thought in his head. "Erik, President Roosevelt said you are someone I can trust and someone who is capable. I'm looking forward to working with you."

Erik nodded in appreciation, and Eisenhower and Beetle walked off.

"Well, now, what an interesting turn of events," Miller said in a condescending tone. "There's only one question we need to ask, isn't there?"

Erik stood apathetic as Miller continued to mock him.

"Will your changes work?"

"General, you've said all that needs to be said. We all have our roles, and I've been given mine. I suggest we focus our energy on making Operation Overlord a success and defeating the Nazis."

"Major, do you know where The Fumoir is?"

"No, sir."

"I'm sure a taxi driver will know," Miller said in a supremely confident tone. "I will be there at 1900 hours."

CHAPTER 16

STRANGE QUIET

"When a good man is hurt, all who would be called good must suffer with him."

— Euripides

LONDON, ENGLAND, THE FUMOIR

The room was full of people murmuring, talking, and laughing. Somebody shouted from the bar, trying to grab someone's attention, while the silverware clinked against one another and scraped on dishes. Solid doors swung open and closed as bussers brought back dirty dishes and glasses, and servers took orders and barked at the kitchen staff. Erik's mouth watered as the perfectly cooked and seasoned steak and seafood steam filled the room. As he passed tables, the aromas of rich caramel beer and robust fruit wines filled his nose. In many ways, it was like the war was not going on. Things rationing should have made inaccessible seemed readily available in The Fumoir.

As Erik walked through the crowd of people, looking at every aspect of the restaurant, he analyzed everything, as if he were a salmon moving upstream. It was faint, but Erik heard his name being called, and he scanned the room like a sniper looking for his target. Nearby, he found Miller with two ladies at a table in the middle of the room, motioning him to join and signaling a server to bring two bottles of wine and another glass. Erik was never into nightclubs or crowded restaurants unless he was in the corner, especially during World War Two with Operation Overlord only days away.

Erik sat amongst the sea of strangers enjoying their time. The boisterous crowd was infectious, but Erik was aware there could be a shark looking for blood in the water, eavesdropping on conversations of high-ranking officers, so he couldn't fully relax.

Erik took a seat as the server returned with the wine and glass. The ladies gazed at Erik candidly, and one shot a knowing wink at him. Miller poured wine into everyone's glasses, then raised his own and looked at Erik with a congenial smile. As Erik nodded, he wondered if going along with the sudden frivolity would make working with Miller easier. Perhaps the general would learn to trust him in the more casual setting, making it easier for them to work together.

"Ladies, I would like you to raise your glass to Eisenhower's newest BTO, Brigadier General Erik Foge." The ladies looked to Miller for an explanation. "I apologize," he replied with a cunning look of gratification on his face, then let out a chuckle before he continued. "It means a *big-time operator*, or, in basic terms, someone who thinks he is important."

Erik glared at Miller and his surroundings as the ladies raised their glasses. The reflection from a lapel pin on a man's suit jacket caught his eyes. He narrowed his attention to the pin as an uneasy feeling, like a spider crawling up his back, overcame him. The pin matched the one worn by the man walking by as Erik entered The Royal Historic Conservatory—an alligator's maw around a Venus flytrap in gold on black. The man raised his glass and nodded at Erik.

"Henry, could you please lower your voice?"

"You address me as sir or general. I am still your superior officer," Miller demanded as he refilled his glass and took a large gulp. "Erik, what's the big deal? The entire world will know soon enough that you are Eisenhower's military strategist." He took another sip. "You are the brainchild of the entire operation." Miller picked up the bottle of wine. "This is a lousy wine, Erik. But not for long, huh?" He filled up Erik's glass. "Because of you, Erik, we will soon down the best French wine. What do you say, Erik?"

Miller raised his glass again and took another sip. "Because you are Eisenhower's most brilliant military strategist, I reckon, it'll only take four days to get from the beaches to Paris." Miller cocked his head. "We'll be there on the tenth."

"General Miller," Erik said in nearly a growl, "I do not know what you're talking about. Sir, you need to button your damn lip. You are drawing too much attention."

"Like you were in the library with that goddamn letter. Miller paused and peered down at Erik, then sarcastically apologized. "Oh, I'm sorry, General. That's right, Prime Minister Churchill and President Roosevelt hold you in such high regard."

Erik stood and confronted Miller. "I'll be damned if I'm going to let you mock me. This isn't the place to talk politics."

Miller stuck his finger in Erik's face. "You need to watch your bearing and stay in your lane. Remember who you're talking to. I'm your superior officer, regardless of your promotion by Eisenhower."

"Major General, you may be my superior officer, but you are also drunk. Did you damn well forget your responsibilities as a senior officer, Henry?"

The ladies excused themselves.

Miller snapped back. "I told you: you address me as sir or general."

Erik shook his head. "Henry, you're a goddamned drunk and acting like an idiot. Just button it up."

Miller's face grew red and pinched with resentment. He got in Erik's face and spoke through his teeth. "I'll have you court-martialed."

"Henry, you're cranky and fussy, and you can ride me on my last nerve, but you have an Achilles Heel. However, you can't help trying to fix what you have already broken."

As Erik made his way out, he noticed the man with the lapel pen had disappeared. A flash from a camera temporally blinded him. Once his eyes adjusted, he quickly looked for the individual with a camera. No luck. Erik took a deep breath and slowly exhaled as he called for a taxi. After climbing in, he ordered the driver to his hotel.

From the shadows, a man emerged and motioned to a nearby car to follow the taxi. As it drove off, another man appeared, his lapel pen reflecting the moonlight, the alligator's head emerging from the water. The first man handed him a roll of film, then they went their separate ways.

CHAPTER 17

BETWEEN THE HEARTBEATS

"There are no disasters. Just opportunities we haven't found yet."
— Vince Flynn, *Lethal Agent*

LONDON, ENGLAND, JUNE 1, 1944

It was a foggy morning in London, with thick, cold fog drifting across the Thames. It drifted up and down the streets and sidewalks, making travel difficult. Erik heard distant foghorns as he pushed his way through the doors of Claridge's to the car waiting for him. He leaped into the backseat of the sedan, and his eyes slowly adjusted. As they neared the river, the overwhelming odor of oil and rotten fish permeated the interior of the car, assaulting Erik's senses and causing his eyes to water. He had a hard time concentrating. The driver advised him they were approximately ten minutes away from Widewing.

They came to a stop at an intersection with a red light, the driver patiently waiting to make a right-hand turn. The light changed to green, and the car lurched forward. Erik glanced to the left as they turned. A delivery truck was bearing down on them at highway speeds, seemingly oblivious of the red light it was approaching. Erik opened his mouth to shout a warning to the driver, but before he could say anything, the world exploded with the sounds of crumpling metal and shattering windows. Hundreds of shards of glass spread through the vehicle like shrapnel from a grenade. As the car spun, tires screeching against the pavement, Erik and his driver were tossed around like laundry in a dryer. Erik braced himself as the car spun. The vehicle came to a rest across both lanes. Another car maneuvered around the wreck only to smash through a nearby storefront.

Erik's ears were ringing so loud he could hear nothing else, but the thudding of his pulse in his temples told him he was still alive. The driver didn't seem as lucky, motionless as blood matted his hair and dripped down onto his uniform.

As the ringing faded, Erik heard sirens and bells from fire trucks. A large man was trying to pull open the rear driver's side door. Others tried to help but failed. Before long, the fire department showed up, and police blocked off the road to prevent any more accidents and guided traffic around the wrecks. Firefighters, with crowbars, Halligan tools, and other equipment headed toward the car.

A firefighter leaned through the window as the others got to work at the door. "Hey, what's your name, mate?"

Erik mumbled his name with a half-dazed look.

"Erik, my name is Johnny. You're going to be alright. Erik, are you hurt anywhere?"

Erik pointed to his shoulder and head.

"Okay, Erik, you are going to be alright. I'm sure you'll be okay." Metal creaked and whined as the other firefighters pried the door open. "Erik, you are going to be okay. You're going to be fine. We're going to get you out of here. Just hang on, okay? Everything will be fine." The firefighter walked to his commanding officer.

Erik overheard him saying an ambulance was on the way and

the driver was dead. Once the door opened, they stabilized his neck and pulled him out of the vehicle, then laid him down just as the ambulance pulled up.

The paramedics rushed over to Erik with a stretcher. They placed Erik on it and secured him inside the ambulance. One of the medics got in the back with Erik while the driver made his way to his seat.

Within moments, the ambulance was charging down the street. Headlights glowing in the fog outside the rear windows converged in a wild and dizzying merry-go-round. The ambulance raced through the mist, sirens wailing. The medic gently placed a cotton cloth over Erik's nose and mouth. "Sir, take deep breaths. Remain calm. We are headed to the hospital."

Erik's hand was restrained. He tried to move his head, but the man kept a firm grip on his forehead and on the cloth. "Sir, you need to remain calm. You could injure yourself further. You were in a serious accident."

Erik had to remember that medicine differed greatly from 2008, where he came from. He struggled to keep his eyes open, but darkness engulfed him as he lost consciousness.

CHAPTER 18

METHOD ONE: A CRISIS OF REVELATION

"Blissful unconsciousness became a foggy awareness which transitioned into painful reality."

— Andy Weir, *The Martian*

Erik slowly opened his eyes, squinting to sharpen the blurred images before him, as a pungent smell of hospital disinfect invaded his nostrils. He was in a room by himself, and his labored breathing and muffled sounds from out in the hallway, such as one would often hear in hospitals, broke the silence. As Erik scanned the deserted, blue and white hospital room, he felt utterly isolated.

Out of impulse, Erik moved his hand to his forehead, touching a pained area on his left temple. His head throbbed, and he realized there was a bandage wrapped around it. He applied some pressure and flinched in pain. He tried to get up and instantly fell back onto the bed. Staring at the ceiling, illuminated by a white, fluorescent light, Erik closed his eyes and took several deep breaths. His mind was thrown into overload as he got his bearings.

He remembered the accident, being pulled out, and blacking out in an ambulance. However, he had more questions than answers. *Where am I? How did I get here? Who was in the ambulance? How long have I been in the hospital?* He was hoping and waiting for some of the hospital staff to come in so they could fill him in on what had happened.

A handsome man with neatly trimmed blond hair and mesmerizing cobalt eyes, wearing a white lab coat over a US Army uniform with the rank of colonel, emerged from the door and interrupted Erik's thought process. Erik tried to get up, but the man prevented him. His name tag read *Dr. Rob Taylor.* The doctor comforted Erik by rubbing his shoulders and pouring him some water. Dr. Taylor placed the pillow under Erik's back so he could sit up. He took a sip of water, and Taylor placed the cup on a bedside table by a radio.

"What happened? How the hell did I get here?" Erik asked.

"Erik," Taylor looked into his eyes, "just take it easy. You are not in danger, I assure you."

"Where am I?" Erik tried to get off the bed, but Taylor restrained him.

"You're in a US Army hospital outside London. I'm an Army doctor. My name is Dr. Rob Taylor." He patted Erik's back and continued with a warm smile, "You can call me Rob."

"What day is it? I need to speak to General Eisenhower."

"I will explain everything to you later, but right now, you just relax. You've been through a lot today. You have a traumatic brain injury. You hit your head pretty hard in the accident." Rob made Erik drink some more water. "We want to make sure nothing serious has happened to your brain." He helped Erik lie down and took a seat next to him. "Now, listen, let's just try a few questions first. Do you remember your name and rank?"

Erik took a deep breath and slowly exhaled. "Brigadier General Erik Foge."

Rob smiled and was pleased as he continued. "Do you remember how old you are?" Rob touched Erik's wedding ring. "Your wife's name?"

"Fifty-three and Jamie Lynn Foge."

"That's good. Very good." He gave more water to Erik. "What's the last thing you remember? Where were you?"

"I remember being placed in an ambulance, and a man placed a piece of cloth over my mouth and nose, and then I blacked out."

"What were you doing?"

"Well, I was picked up at the hotel and was being driven to SHAEF Headquarters."

There was a subtle knock at the door before it opened to reveal a lieutenant general, who offered a warm smile and a gentle wave.

"How is Erik doing, doctor?"

"General, considering what he has been through this morning, he is lucky to be alive. The other doctors were concerned about his brain injury and his memory. I will let them know the good news. He has no memory loss."

"Eisenhower will be pleased to hear that. Do you mind if I take Erik outside? We need to discuss some matters, and a little fresh air might do him good."

"I wouldn't disagree with that," Rob said as he stood up, then he turned to Erik. "If you keep going as you are, I should be able to release you back to work in no time. I'll get some lunch ordered for you. It should be here by the time you get back. I'm sure you are starving."

Erik nodded, noticing it was nearly noon.

Outside, a landscape of manicured lawns, bushes, and gardens surrounded Erik. The hospital was composed of six white, Victorian buildings that were stunning yet homey with their ornate woodwork. Staff members walked with patients engaged in outdoor activities. The general placed his hand in front of Erik before he crossed the driveway, stopping him short just as a jeep pulled up.

"Sorry, General," the driver called out after he slammed on the brakes.

"It's okay, Sergeant. Be a little more careful."

"Yes, sir."

They exchanged salutes, and after the jeep pulled away, Erik and the general continued walking. Erik glanced over his shoulder at the vehicle as it drove off, noticing it had only a white star but not the circle added for those in the European theater. He continued, his head throbbing at the temples. He looked past the hospital buildings to rolling hills with thick evergreen trees that were such a dark green they were almost black. The sky was grayish white with patches of darkness and low hovering clouds that appeared poised to burst at any minute.

As soon as the general and Erik were at a distance from everyone, he spoke. "Erik, we are glad you are well. Eisenhower was worried. Forgive me for getting ahead of myself. My name is Lieutenant General Russell Thorson. I work with Eisenhower." He held out his hand to greet Erik with a proper introduction. He then reached into his pocket and pulled out a cigarette holder and a small leather box, approximately the size of a small jewelry box, which he gave to Erik. "Congratulations, Erik."

"What's this?" Erik opened the box, saw two silver stars, and glanced up at Thorson, wondering what was going on.

"Your newly promoted rank. Eisenhower thinks you will be a very valuable asset. He wanted to make sure everything you said at the briefing was accurate."

Erik nodded.

"Good. He would like you to give the briefing to King George and Queen Elizabeth in two days.

"Can I ask why, sir?"

Thorson lit his cigarette, took a deep drag, and he looked with pleasure at Erik's rapt expression. He exhaled, blue smoke leaving his nostrils, and held his cigarette in a peculiar way, between the tips of his thumb and index finger. He motioned for Erik to take a seat on a nearby bench. "I really don't know why, but Eisenhower wants to make sure you can remember everything before then." He cupped Erik's shoulder. "As you know, you have gone through a lot, but we have to make sure everything turns out well for you and the landings. A lot is at stake here."

Some ash fell off the end of Thorson's cigarette onto his jacket, and he brushed it off. He took another drag of the cigarette and spoke through the smoke. "What do you remember?"

Erik took a deep breath as he racked his brain, and suddenly he remembered that Europeans held their cigarettes like the general was. As Erik tried to think straight, a sudden pain throbbed in his temple, the pain expanding to his forehead, causing his eyes to water. He pressed his palms to his temples. He felt as if a metal vise were being tightened around his head. He shielded his eyes to avoid looking directly at the light, which intensified the pain.

Thorson quickly glanced around and motioned to a nurse to assist them. She grabbed the nearest wheelchair and headed in their direction.

Once inside, Erik was taken to his room and laid on his bed. The nurse helped Erik drink some water as Dr. Taylor offered some aspirin, which Erik swallowed. The doctor asked the nurse to help Erik eat so he could gain his strength, and then to make sure he got some rest. Erik asked for the radio to be on so he could relax to some music. Taylor agreed.

Dr. Taylor and Thorson walked out into the hallway and headed to Taylor's office. Once there, Taylor closed the door behind them, and each grabbed a seat. General Thorson sat back in his chair and rested his elbows on the arms. He glanced down at the dial of his wristwatch, then interlaced the fingers of both his hands like a teacher preparing to listen to a long explanation. He glared at Taylor and said, "We need to make sure he remembers the information about the landings, or it will cost us the war."

The office telephone purred softly. Thorson picked up the receiver, listened briefly, and said, "Yes, sir, I realize how critical the situation we are in." He nodded. "Yes, sir, he is with me now, and we were talking about that when you called. Yes, sir, I will." He returned the receiver and glared at Taylor.

Taylor felt he should defend himself and his department and was determined to get his message through. "I'm very aware of our situation, and that the invasion will happen in the next couple of days." Taylor stood up motionless and erect, as inscrutable as a parrot, and looked thoughtfully at General Thorson with his dark, slanting, cobalt eyes. "I will not fail."

General Thorson crossed the room and walked out, closing the door softly behind him.

A moment later, Taylor walked out of his office, headed to Erik's room, and was stopped by a nurse, who informed him Erik was sleeping. He gave the nurse instructions to check on Erik hourly and to inform him when he awakened.

***

Erik awoke, slowly tilted back his head, and gazed into the nothingness of the ceiling with the blur of fluorescent light. He turned his head and blinked several times until his bloodshot eyes, with strain, focused. He stared across the table at the radio playing "*I'll Get By (As Long as I Have You)*" by Harry James and His Orchestra with Dick Haymes. He reached over and attempted to turn off the radio. In a futile attempt, he accidentally knocked the radio off the table, and it shattered on the floor. Erik climbed out and sat on the floor, picking up the pieces. He lowered his head and looked over each piece individually, and something flickered for an instant before his inquisitive eyes. He blinked and examined the piece of wood. His eyes widened as he read the bold black letters: *Hergestellt in Deutschland.* Made in Germany. He quickly jumped to his feet, located his clothes, and got dressed. A knock came at the door as he was placing his shoes on. He quickly finished tying them, got up while picking up a piece of wood, and faced the window.

"Sir, I brought your dinner." The orderly looked around, noticing the radio was broken as he placed the tray down. "Sir, what happened here?"

"Close the door and come here. I need your opinion on something I'm looking at."

Erik took a deep breath, held it, and slowly exhaled as his mind focused on the next problem: escaping. Erik used the window as a mirror, and once the orderly was close, he attacked. First, Erik threw the piece of wood at the orderly's face to distract him. The man raised his hands up to shield his face, leaving his temples open, and Erik hit them both. The orderly stumbled back, dazed, as he attempted to prepare himself to fight. Erik struck a blow to the orderly's gut, then another to his jaw, resulting in a satisfying crunch of shattered bone. The orderly raised his hands to protect his face, and Erik unleashed several thundering jabs at the man's ribcage, cracking several ribs. He struck the orderly's jaw again, dislocating it entirely. The orderly collapsed, his attempts to call out for help coming out as nothing more than a pitiful whimper through his shattered and displaced jaw.

Erik took stock of his situation. He was outnumbered and outgunned, and it was probable that nobody knew where he was. Hell, *he* didn't know where he was. He needed to focus on escaping the building. He couldn't let fear or panic break his focus on the task at hand. In a matter of minutes, he might have a dozen men with Mauser rifles and MP40 submachine guns on his tail. He had to keep moving and only fight when necessary. His primary objectives were to stay alive, avoid injury, and get the hell out.

Erik knew there had to be a side entrance, so he headed to the end of the hallway and found a staircase. He opened the door quietly, stepped through, and eased it closed. He composed himself as he raced down the stairs. Not far from the stairwell was the side entrance he was looking for, guarded by two military policemen. Erik nodded to them and strode confidently through the door as if he were going for a leisurely stroll in a park. He walked down some steps to a broad terrace and started walking toward the back of the building.

"Sir, are you a patient here?" one of the MPs called out as he headed toward Erik. The other spoke into a hand-held radio, trying to obtain additional information. "Sir, can I get your name?" the first called out again.

Erik knew that depending on what he said or his body language, the guard could get the drop on him. In training, they taught him to ignore them, walk away, and once they're in the distance, he can get a drop on them. "Sir, identify yourself."

The MP placed his hand on Erik's shoulder and squeezed firmly. Erik stopped for a moment, then ducked and spun around, then unleashed a focused strike on the MP's ribcage. As the man stumbled back, Erik punched him in the throat. As the first MP gasped for air, Erik ran and slid under the other MP like a baseball player sliding home, kicking upward to topple the man over. Once he was on the ground, Erik hammered his elbow to his chest several times. He then grabbed the guard's pistol from his holster and stood in silence with two unconscious MPs at his feet.

Suddenly, an alarm blasted from all corners of the compound. Erik sprinted across the lush green lawn, looking for an exit because climbing the fence would take too much time. In the distance, he saw a guard post, and beyond that was a road and a forest. Once inside the forest, he would have somewhat of an advantage from the cover, but he had to get there first. As he neared the exit, two soldiers came out of the guard post, turning to Erik with their fingers on the triggers of their weapons. As they raised their weapons to aim, Erik already had them in his sights and killed each of them with a single bullet to the chest.

He stole an MP40 from one of the dead guards. A sudden hail of bullets peppered the ground around him, and Erik dove into the guard booth as they sent up plumes of dirt. A dozen soldiers armed with rifles and submachine guns ran after him, all firing their weapons. Erik leaned out from the guard post, sending bullets from the MP40 ripping through the courtyard, hitting several soldiers while the others dove for cover.

Once the clip was empty, Erik ran from the guard booth, turned, and wove down the road to avoid being hit, heading toward the trees as fast as his feet would carry him. The soldiers behind him were closing in, trying to outflank him. Several engines roared from down the road, and he headed toward them, hoping to steal a vehicle to make his escape.

Unfortunately for Erik, he turned a bend in the forested road to find it blocked by three Opel Blitz trucks, all disgorging armed soldiers who fanned out to take cover in the trees. Behind Erik, several vehicles and more men poured out of the hospital grounds.

Erik dashed to the woods, but soldiers armed with MP40s blocked his way as others closed in behind him. Erik raised his pistol to his head, but a sniper must have been watching and removed the pistol from Erik's hand in one shot. The soldiers made way for a Kübelwagen. A man wearing a black SS uniform displaying the rank of major general approached Erik with his Lugar drawn. As he neared, Erik recognized the man who just recently presented himself as Lieutenant General Russell Thorson.

"The true uniform comes out," Erik stated, and the general smirked. "I knew this would come sooner or later."

"We know who you are, and now you know who we are." The

general grinned sadistically as his eyes narrowed. He allowed the significance of his remarks to sink in.

Erik chuckled and shook his head. He stared into the general's eyes. "So, this whole thing was a charade? It was a little melodramatic for my tastes. Why didn't you kill me?"

One of the soldiers struck Erik in the back of the leg with the butt of his weapon, forcing him to his knees. The SS general stood over him, barely deigning to tilt his head as he looked down his nose at his captive. "You know I owe you no explanation. My business was to detain you from escaping. I do not control the other part. Let's just leave it at that."

With that, one of the soldiers dragged a hood over Erik's head. As the smell of ether filled his nostrils, the world faded once again to darkness.

CHAPTER 19

MADNESS ONE: THE FEELING BEGINS

"Sigh… okay. I've had my tantrum and now I have to figure out
how to stay alive." — Andy Weir, *The Martian*

Erik awoke in a six-by-six cell, where cold, quiet, and emptiness
came together. It was a world unto itself. The floor and walls were
cold, coarse concrete with a damp residue. He was greeted by a
blinding light coming from the door that was so bright that it
pierced his eyes. Due to not having a wristwatch, Erik did not
realize if he had slept for minutes or hours, so he had no idea what
time of day it was. To make matters worse, he did not know what
day it was.

Erik did know several things. They were going to try to get
information from him. They would do anything and everything
to lower his defenses. There would be no compromise, and there
was nothing he could do but resist. The days would be long, his
mind would be working overtime, and he needed to keep his body
strong. Until they came to get him, there was nothing he could do
to prepare. The survival, evasion, resistance, and escape instructors
taught Erik that during the time he spent in isolation, he had to
keep positive, cling to the past, and embrace the inevitability that
as soon as the door opened, things would not be pleasant. In such

an uncertain situation, Erik knew that stress was likely to consume him in the long run. The question was, would he control it, or would it control him?

Because of Erik's SERE training, he understood that a sense of normalcy would begin to wane as he was tortured. This was simply because torture puts both mental and physical strain on the individual. The first time, one might think it was horrific, but they could survive it. The second time, one shivers from pain and tries to remain strong. Finally, if one made it through the third round, they were often left cowering and squatting in the corner of their cell, wishing it would end. The hard part was the spans of time between torture sessions, because that was all mental.

Erik expected to be beaten, bound in contorted stress positions, and subjected to deafening noise. Sleep disruption to the point of hallucination would follow, along with deprivation of food, drink, and medical care for wounds, and possibly subjection to extreme heat or cold. Erik experienced all these in SERE training, but still wondered if he could endure. He knew moving forward, the unraveling of his psyche would begin, and the SS would do anything to break him down. If he lived to talk about it, Erik knew he would never be the same. There would be a transition as the torture methods and isolation led to madness. The time between method and madness was what he feared most.

The blinding light slowly faded to nothing, and Erik felt the darkness consume him. His eyes opened wide as footsteps echoed in the stone corridor that led to his cell door. Then came the clanking of a guard trying to find the right key and the grinding of the tumblers as they placed the key in the keyhole. The rusty metal lock was grated. The door creaked open. Then, three SS men stood at the entrance, two with MP40s raised. The other circled around Erik. He knew he could take them, but they might shoot and injure him, and that would not be beneficial to his escape.

The light from the hallway burned his eyes just before they placed a shroud over his head. They took him out of the cell, and he knew he was being taken to an interrogation room. It is with good reason that people shake in fear at mention of the SS. Their reputation for how they gather information was chilling. Erik prepared himself for the loaded questions they were going to ask, demand answers, and their assurances it would be in Erik's best interest to respond. In other words, they were going to tell him how to behave as their guest.

Erik would resist. He would do his best, even knowing the SS would push him to his limits and beyond. He could not answer their questions. The only thing Erik could do was keep his spirit unbroken and not be deterred.

CHAPTER 20

METHOD TWO: INHALE, EXHALE, NOTHING TO SAY

"If you won't do anything, I will."

— Elijah Mikaelson, *The Originals*

The room was damp, and the quiet was broken only by Erik's breathing and the groaning of the wooden seat on which he sat. He was bound to a chair, and escape was impossible. Again, he was blinded by a bright light until the silhouette of a man appeared. He looked at Erik's face with suspicious bewilderment, his eyes filled with dark portents. The man's breath smelled of coffee.

"Erik, we know so much about you, yet we know very little about you at all, General Foge."

"Erik Foge, brigadier general, serial number O-2400396."

A solid punch to Erik's jaw sent a snarl of agony over his face. "That's to make sure you are paying attention." The interrogator exhaled. "We're going to be here as long as it takes. Let's start off with something easy now."

Erik knew the interrogator was trying to gather information from him. Even if it was something simple, it would be something they had to know for their future operations. So, regardless of how basic the information was, the best thing to do was to play dumb and not respond. With what Erik knew about the future, anything he said could have catastrophic consequences.

"You'll tell me everything you know." A cunning grin appeared on the man's face. "Perhaps I can convince you to cooperate with little suffering." The interrogator stared at Erik, waiting for a response. "It looks like it's going to be a longer session."

Taking a deep breath, Erik leaned back against the chair and prepared himself for what was to come.

"When did you find out that you were not in England?"

Erik looked up and said nothing.

The man slapped him across the face. "Tell me." Another slap, to the other side. His face started swelling as warm, wet dripped from his nose and a sharp stinging pain blossomed between the eyes. The coppery taste of blood filled his mouth. Erik said nothing.

"When." A slap to the left. "Did." A slap to the right. "You." A slap to the left. "Find." A slap to the right. "Out." A slap to the left. "That." A slap to the right. "You." A slap to the left. "Were." A slap to the right. "Not." A slap to the left. "In." A slap to the right. "England." A slap to the left. The interrogator walked behind Erik and stopped. "Just tell me."

Then, without warning, Erik's head was suddenly jerked backward, revealing the delicate esophagus, trachea, and larynx in his neck, and the man flicked a finger against Erik's Adam's apple, causing him to gasp and choke. "The truth," the interrogator insisted.

Erik gasped for air as pain rippled through his throat. The interrogator sprang around and grasped Erik's neck and squeezed with a strong, vice-like grip. Small, ragged gasps escaped Erik's throat. As the man spoke in a menacing tone, he leaned forward and looked into Erik's stained eyes. "We're going to be here as long as it takes. You don't need to make this even more difficult for yourself." The interrogator smiled as he pulled out his Lugar, studying it before looking back at Erik.

Erik was panting. Fresh bruises discolored his disoriented, tortured face as dirt, sweat, and blood dripped from it.

The interrogator rubbed the barrel of the pistol up and around Erik's temple. "It would be a very poor decision on your part if you didn't give me the information I need." In a calming voice, he asked again. "When did you find out that you were not in England?"

Seeing Erik's rage, the interrogator nodded, indicating it was okay to share the information.

Erik nodded back. "You are asking when I found out that I was not in England?" He snickered. The interrogator looked at someone behind him. Erik looked over and directed his next statement to the figure hiding in the shadows. "Hi, there. Lovely place you have here."

A flare of pain ripped across Erik's face from the interrogator's palm. "Focus."

Erik looked into his eyes.

"This is a simple question. All I need to know is how."

Erik nodded and snickered again. "How?" Erik shook his head. "I won't even tell you that, no matter what you do."

The interrogator raised his authoritarian voice with an accusatory finger pointed at Erik. "Even if you don't give us what we want to know, there will be another officer, who will be weaker, who will provide us with the information." The interrogator lightly slapped Erik once more. "Give me what I need, and I will stop."

Erik shook his head and got slapped again.

"I suggest you do it soon, before my superiors change their minds about keeping you alive."

Erik just stared at him

The interrogator shook his head. "You're not really aren't going to tell me."

Erik shook his head and replied. "Erik Foge, brigadier general, serial number O-2400396."

With all his frustration, the interrogator pistol-whipped the Lugar across Erik's head and kicked the chair over with him in it, then stated in a sinister tone, "Round two."

The interrogator snapped his fingers, and a few guards cut the ropes binding Erik. They turned him to face the wall. As they stretched Erik like a crucified man, they placed a biting block in his mouth while a coarse rope sliced into his skin. His facial muscles twitched nervously as he expected the worst, and his eyes took on a haunted look. His ears tried to pick up any noise that would indicate what was to happen next.

The interrogator briefly stepped into the spotlight, revealing the rank of sturmscharführer, or storm section leader. Despite the short height and stocky build of the sturmscharführer, he was well-muscled and looked like he was chiseled from an artist's block. He had the presence of a National Football League running back. In the shadows, he reached for something on a table and then brought a coiled bullwhip into the light. He gripped the handle, which was swallowed up by his massive hand.

"I'm giving you a chance before we move on." The sturmscharführer placed the whip in Erik's peripheral vision. "Have you thought any more about it?"

Erik's heart pounded through his chest as sweat ran down his face. He took a deep breath, tilted his head, and nodded. "I have."

The sturmscharführer grinned.

"And I'm sorry, but I just don't feel like talking."

The grin faded, and the sturmscharführer took several steps back. Once within striking distance, his movements became a fluid and graceful display of strength, poise, and balance. The sturmscharführer's talent with the bullwhip made his arm and whip appear to be one, as if they were extensions of each other. Then, suddenly, he swung the whip, lashing the air, and its crack echoed throughout the room as it tore apart Erik's skin, leaving a bloody gash as a river of blood running down Erik's back.

"Do you want to share any specific information?"

Erik breathed deeply. Then, the bullwhip lashed out against his back, then again, one after another. His body roiled in pain and his hands balled up into tight fists, his knuckles turning whiter after each lash.

"Do you have anything to say?" The Sturmscharführer snarled. "All I need is for you to tell me when you found out you were not in England, and I will stop."

"Fuck you!" Erik barked back as his body stiffened in apprehension of the next lashing. Then, he felt a cool liquid on his back, followed by a sudden burning. It was rubbing alcohol. It ran down the crevasses of his back. Erik cringed as the icy rubbing alcohol saturated his wounds. It felt like the wounds were being pulled apart or burning. His eyes watered from the pain as he tightened every muscle in his body. Then, the sturmscharführer ground salt into his wounds, every grain feeling like tiny needles as they were jammed deeper into his wounds.

Erik's voice exploded with agony and his eyes clamped shut. He took shallow breaths as a voice yelled in his head. *Do not think about the pain! Do not give in to the pain! You adjust for it! You make minor adjustments!* Erik looked over his shoulder, and his eyes took on a possessed look as he stared at the sturmscharführer with a wicked grin. "I will have my vengeance, I promise you."

Once again, the sturmscharführer grabbed the whip and gripped the handle fiercely. He stared at Erik, and after a few moments, he swung the whip, sending the tip lashing through the air. The imbrued tip ate away at Erik's flesh like a shark attacking its prey. Pain ramped up from his side and continued across his abdomen as the blinding agony intensified. A burst of pain flared up every time the sturmscharführer made contact. Blood ran down his sides as pain crawled across his back. The figure standing in the shadows motioned for the sturmscharführer to stop and cut the ropes.

Erik's body thumped across the floor. More pain crashed through his body, and he gasped as two SS guards with MP40s hovered over him. The sturmscharführer stood over him, smirking and shaking his head. Erik's predatory expression grew as the sturmscharführer stepped on his left hand and applied pressure, causing every bone to grind together and straining ligaments, tendons, and muscles. All Erik could do was glance up and grin through the pain as he glared at the SS non-commissioned officer.

"Stand up." The sturmscharführer demanded.

Erik struggled to get up and took several deep breaths. Once he was upright, the interrogator delivered a blow to his gut, causing Erik to bow from the pain. "Look at me, you piece of—"

Without hesitation, Erik struck with a flattened palm at the sturmscharführer's nasal bone, driving it up into the man's brain. His lifeless body dropped to the floor before the man had a chance to realize what was happening. The SS guards smashed the butts of their weapons on Erik's back, forcing him onto his knees, and quickly restrained him.

From the shadows, an SS colonel with glowering, cobalt eyes appeared. Erik recognized him as Dr. Rob Taylor. The man stared into Erik's eyes and drooled, "I know so little about who you are." He observed Erik as he continued. "Do you wonder who I am?" He paused for a moment, knowing Erik would not answer. "Your child-like behavior tells me I will have to step up my game. I won't kill you… yet."

The SS colonel kicked Erik's jaw. "He might not have broken you, but in time, I will take everything from you." He gave a sadistic grin. "Be aware that your wretched existence will continue only by my will. You will beg me to sweep away your pain and the shards of your shattered, pathic, insignificant life. You will spend the last days of your life wishing you were dead. Death will offer more peace than I can, but until that time, you are nothing to me, and I will get the information I need."

Erik spat out a mouthful of blood and looked up with defiance burning in his eyes. "I want you to know I will strive every day just to stay alive, and though I may be on the verge of death, I'll be satisfied simply to know you will fail."

"Some people would call my methods evil." The colonel squinted as he continued. "I consider them an efficient performance of my job. I never fail." The colonel stared down at Erik. "I can look inside you and know what you are thinking. I know you are thinking, 'Do your 'worst.' And I already have an answer for you." He spoke through his teeth. "I *always* do."

Erik shook his head as the colonel motioned him to continue. He said calmly, "I have three kinds of people in my life. Friends, enemies, and people I have killed. You will be in the last column."

"Don't count on it," the colonel scoffed. "The way I see it, you are at a great disadvantage."

Then, everything went black.

CHAPTER 21

MADNESS TWO: FEELING COLD AND ALONE

"Time will not slow down when something unpleasant lies ahead."

— J. K. Rowling, *Harry Potter and the Goblet of Fire*

Tossed back like a piece of trash to the curb, Erik's clothes were soaked with water. In his cell, the darkness consumed him as his wet clothes absorbed the frigid temperature and raided his body's heat. At the Farm, Erik recalled, they taught him survival, evasion, resistance, and escape training, and the instructor advised him, as a paramilitary operations officer, that he might experience extreme isolation. Erik had prepared himself to constantly face difficult situations. He knew torture would be extremely stressful and difficult, and worse case, they could kill him.

As long as that doesn't happen, Erik needed to focus on escaping and returning to friendly units and ensure his physical and mental well-being upon returning. Erik knew there were five basic conditions that could affect his survival. However, he only needed to focus on four of the five, all of which would affect his survival.

The first one was environmental conditions. It could refer either to being held captive or an outdoor environment; regardless, neither extreme cold nor high temperatures are pleasing. What most people didn't realize is that one loses a lot of their body heat through their head. Erik removed his shirt, wrapped it around his head, and curled up in a fetal position to keep his body heat close. With being isolated, there are four things to consider about one's well-being. They are physical condition, psychological effectiveness, material needs, and legal and moral obligations. The fourth one didn't apply to Erik's situation. In situations like his, most people, if they're educated, might bring up there are legal obligations identified in the Geneva Conventions or the Uniform Code of Military Justice. However, when dealing with the SS, that won't matter because they're determined to get the information they need, and Erik would die before giving them anything.

While in isolation, there are tons of psychological effects Erik was experiencing. In addition to the ones mentioned previously, he also experienced lack of rest, lack of access to food, and lack of water. In time, he knew the SS would provide him with low-protein food, it would allow them to control him more easily by brainwashing him. Also, the SS were hoping the following would occur to Erik being in isolation. One, he would grow insecure, which is induced by anxiety and self-doubts. Two and three went hand in hand because they're often induced by coercive manipulation. Number two was a loss of self-esteem and three was a loss of self-determination. Because of the importance of these two for Erik's survival, he had to have the will to survive, his most important tool. He was also taught to focus on feelings of obligation or responsibilities to family, self, and spiritual beliefs. He was trained to think of positive thoughts; however, sometimes, it did not work.

The temperature dropped again, and the blinding light was ever-present. Even though the first interrogation was over, Erik knew the struggle would continue between him and the SS. So, when he was alone, would he be able to see who controls who?

The SS would have complete control, and they were very effective at breaking people to make them confess or talk. However, it was Erik's forward progress that required him to maintain his control and willpower. He also knew he had to be careful if he showed strength, because they can make things difficult in an instant. Erik told himself he needed to focus on gaining strength and a strong mental attitude. He also considered what he needed to do to survive and how he might escape?

He squinted at the whining of metal as his cell door opened. Then, something soft hit his face, and he cringed as freezing cold water engulfed him like a blanket. The door closed. His body was soaked again. Water dripped from his hair, mixing with blood to run into his eyes and down his chin. Erik fumbled through the dark as his fingers explored his surroundings. He felt something that had a springy texture, yet on the outside edges, it had a flaky, crumbly texture. He sniffed the item, and a slightly sweet and yeasty aroma consumed him. It was a piece of bread. They gave him food, just barely enough to survive. His mouth watered with every bite. Erik removed his shirt from his head and began sucking the water from it.

After eating, Erik tried to fall asleep, but the guards awoke him, kicking his cell door. Sadly, Erik didn't know if he slept for five minutes or five hours. He knew he was being watched, because it happened several times. In an almost incalculable number of ways, it seemed that they were trying to break him in a repetitive and endless manner. They taught Erik in SERE training that he had to control his emotions. This was crucial to strengthen his will to survive, especially when the SS were doing both physical and psychological torture.

There could be no other way to describe their methods and madness than that it seemed to be a physical thing inside of him that affected his whole being. Erik felt the madness was so thick it was like it was choking him. His mind and soul were being drained of sanity and spirit by the torture methods they used, and subsequently, his body was being robbed of life. With those things constantly consuming him, he needed to close his eyes, relax, and analyze the situation rationally.

The first thing he needed to do was to collect his thoughts and clear his mind. Erik knew that in order to survive in such an isolating situation, he would have to decide when and how he would try to escape, as well as the most important decision, whether or not he would stay alive. He knew failure to take this course of action would be considered a decision for inaction. Because of this, a lack of decision-making may have caused his death. The more time he spent as a prisoner, Erik felt hope became less tenable, making it hard to get a hold of. Hope was like sand in an hourglass. The sand disappearing made it increasingly difficult to keep track as the minutes and then hours disappeared while he stayed trapped.

Erik closed his eyes and took several deep breaths. He was recalling the spring of 1945, when Jamie was six months pregnant, and she bought a Victorian deluxe crib that had many wooden parts and screws. A grin came across his face as he recalled Jamie holding up instructions and saying, "See?" Then she pointed to the drawing. "It's going to look like this when I'm finished."

Erik nodded in agreement, giving moral support. "Very nice."

Jamie looked at the instructions and the parts that were spread out with no organization, as she stated in a confused tone, "This thing is going to be bigger than the room by the time I'm finished." She shook her head, realizing the complexity.

"Uh-huh." Erik leaned back in his chair. "Want some help?"

Jamie nodded and smiled. "Yeah, you can hand me the screws and bolts. I think I should divide all these parts into groups to determine their structural function." She tossed the instructions and glanced over her shoulder at Erik. "I'm going need to be in the right mood to do this."

Erik smirks back. "You were a second ago." Erik rubbed his chin as he glanced at the parts of the crib. "I think we should hire someone to put it together."

Erik felt like the cell was getting smaller and smaller until he could stand in one place and touch both walls at the same time. In addition, he didn't know how high the ceiling was, so when he was forced up or even stood up to stretch, he was cautious not to bump his head. Erik felt like he was being buried alive, but his mind was playing tricks on him. There was no furniture in the cell, not even a bed. It is almost impossible to imagine, but Erik was getting used to sleeping on a stone slab, even though he had been there for a short period of time.

As Erik slept, the emotional aspects associated with isolation engulfed him like a blanket. His mind and body were trying to cope and adapt to various physiological and emotional signs, feelings, and expressions affecting him mentally. However, Erik knew he had tolerance limits, both psychological and physical. There were two grave threats to maintaining his positive attitude: comfort and apathy. Both threats represented attitudes that must be avoided at all costs. In the civilian world, comfort was considered a great thing. Yet, when one was isolated, comfort could harm their survival. Erik knew he must value life more than comfort and be willing to endure the psychological torture, hunger, pain, and any other discomfort to give him the motivation to escape.

Like comfort, apathy would determine if one was going to die in isolation or escape and survive. He needed to avoid drowsiness, mental numbness, and indifference, all of which would cause apathy. What Erik was taught in SERE training is that surviving isolation is like staring into the Grim Reaper's abyss when he arrives and shouting, "Fuck you! I'm not ready to die yet! Do your worst…, for I will do mine!"

Erik had to show the Grim Reaper he didn't give a damn about it because the Reaper didn't give a damn about him. In short, success could be achieved by simply not giving up or in.

CHAPTER 22

METHOD THREE: BENDING THE ARC OF FEAR

"The human body was not meant for such abuse."

— John Grisham, *The Firm*

Without warning, Erik gasped, followed by rapid, uncontrollable breathing. His heart rate increased as his skin felt like it was burning, then like needles were penetrating his skin. He felt incredibly weak throughout his body. Then, he got the wind knocked out of him as the SS guards kicked him in the stomach. As he gasped for air, they brought him to his feet and wrapped a rope around his neck like a python. The fibers dug into his skin like teeth on a saw, and blood trickled down his chest. They placed a shroud over his head as they forced his hands behind his back. Unexpectedly, a hard, cutting blow to his gut caught him off guard. It seemed like the guard was a professional boxer from his attack and how the pain exploded across Erik's abs as he doubled over. He received another blow from the same guard, only to get a rabbit punch on the back of the neck. This made him arch back again as he exhaled and fell to the floor.

"Get up." The guard demanded as he kicked Erik in the gut.

He tried to curl into a fetal position, but they jerked him up and dragged him down the hallway. Erik knew things would be like that when he was a part of the O.G.D.S. Team 42 if he were captured. Then, like now, no one knew where he was, no one would miss him, and he would be considered "missing in action". Since the guards weren't walking at his pace, waking up became painful and traumatic. They stepped on his bare feet grazed them as they dragged them over the rough stone. They were bleeding and he almost lost his big toenail. His face sagged as blood dripped from his mouth. He took deep breaths as his heart hammered against his ribs, and his throat tightened as he prepared for what was going to happen next.

The guards stopped.

Creaking metal echoed through Erik's ears. Again, he was dragged. Then he felt completely violated as the guards completely undressed him. He was naked and defenseless. Next, they forced him into a wicker chair. Dried and cracked wickers, which felt like hundreds of tiny scalpels, penetrated Erik's buttocks and back. Erik's hands were bound behind the chair, and his ankles to the front legs. The tightness of the rope left no play in any of the bindings. After a while, the rope tore Erik's flesh open, causing him to bleed as the rope continued to tear into his skin. The chair's legs were broadly spaced, so it would not rock.

As the shroud came off, Erik's eyes slowly adjusted to the poorly lit room, which he quickly analyzed. His nostrils smelled a faint but distinct smell of copper. He knew that could only be one thing: blood. It was not his, but that of others who came before him. The complete picture became clear. Imbrued stones surrounded him. One could describe it as a slaughterhouse. For the first time since his capture, fear of the unknown crawled up Erik's spine. Then, he saw a silhouette of a person in the shadows who was staring in his direction. It was an extremely unpleasant picture. Erik sat naked in the middle of the room. His bruises and the open wounds from the whip ached. His eyes were sunken and bloodshot, and his face was streaked with blood and dirt that barely masked his exhaustion and uncertainty of what was to come.

The individual's wooden heels ground against the stone like nails on a chalkboard. He strolled toward the light, slowly revealing his distinguished black uniform that was emblematic of the rank of an SS Colonel with every step he took. From the shadows, a deep, sinister voice stated, "Good day, General. Or is it night? In this room, it doesn't matter. No time exists in this room." The colonel smirked. "Last time we met was not pleasant. Maybe later, we will treat your wounds, depending on the conversation. If we have a fruitful conversation, your time with me will be short. However," he paused for a moment, "if you decide to employ your American arrogance like last time, this will be a long, unfortunate experience."

As he stepped out of the shadow, the light slowly illuminated his pale complexion and thin lips twisted into a malevolent grin. He had impenetrable, squinting, cobalt eyes which peered down at Erik. He hovered with disdain as he scrutinized Erik like a nineteenth-century pathologist with his medical instruments, studying a newly discovered creature on a dissection table.

Erik stared back and replied with a smug look, "What can I say, I am up for new experiences."

The colonel stood with his arms crossed over his chest and stated with complete apathy, "Fine." Then, his voice turned harshly cold. "Then let's explore these new experiences together. As an intelligence officer, I am sure you know about the beaches in France and Belgium."

"I never went there. I don't go to the beach. The sand gets everywhere, but I heard the sunsets are amazing."

The colonel was obviously not amused. "Erik, let's not be coy. You have the answers I am looking for. Share them, or we start with a new experience together." He smirked.

Erik shook his head. "Sorry, you are not my type. I heard the SS doesn't condone homosexuality. Is that true? If you keep it quiet, maybe you can meet the right guy and experience that. Just don't get caught, like Ernst Röhm."

"This first experience is called *meet the monkey*. If you are wondering why your chair has no bottom in it, it's because that is where the monkey will touch you if you give the wrong answer."

Few men realized how evil Apophis was or knew of his methods. The simple thought of describing this pain was unfathomable, yet Apophis, whose mind was quite twisted compared to others, sized up Erik. Slowly and surely, he drew his plans to break him.

Apophis crossed his arms over his chest. "You presume to know me? Then know this: Whatever I have in store for you, I'm destined to make you suffer in ways your feeble little mind cannot possibly imagine." Apophis leaned forward as he pulled out his dagger. "And when it's over…" He dragged the blade's edge against Erik's face, cutting his facial hair. "You have no idea of what I am capable of doing. If you have something in your mind which I want."

He tapped Erik's head with the blade. "You could render me obsolete by telling me what you know, because I'm a lot worse if I don't get what I want." Apophis straightened his back and noticed Erik's toenail was coming off. He held his SS dagger like a beacon as he moved the razor-sharp tip slowly, relentlessly toward Erik's toe. "You will associate my name with fear and pain." He squatted down and toyed with Erik's toenail with the tip of the dagger. Erik's toe muscles twitched nervously. "Then you realize that…" He removed the toenail and dragged the tip of the dagger across the skin underneath as he looked into Erik's eyes, which darted manically. "You are nothing to me."

Apophis walked to a table as Erik took deep breaths. "Forgive me for not introducing myself. My real name is Dr. Apophis Adelram."

Erik noticed, as before, that he spoke in English with no accent. His voice was low, soft, and firm, as if he had summoned the next patient from the waiting room.

"Oh, come, Erik." He looked at Erik, but there was no emotion in his eyes, which hid his inner evil. "If you give me the information I need, then we'll be able to end this quickly." He grabbed a bottle of rubbing alcohol and approached Erik. "As a medical doctor, I learned about human anatomy and the elaborate tortures that can cause pain."

"You must have an impressive resume with all that knowledge." Erik mocked.

Apophis replied, "I know you have never heard of Dr. Josef Mengele."

Erik tried to remain calm and took deep breaths.

"We in the SS call him the Angel of Death." Apophis grins. "I would like to be the Angel of Pain." He slowly moved the tip of the dagger toward Erik's upper chest. Erik's body tensed up and began to tremble as he tried to turn his head away. Apophis grabbed a handful of hair and held his head still. "It will be less painful if you don't move." The dagger hissed as Apophis dragged it across his chest, the cold steel tip splitting his skin and leaving behind a trail of blood which ran down his chest. He repeated the process five more times as he continued questioning Erik, whose eyes were transfixed with horror, and who let out a guttural scream each time he was cut.

"Where will the landings occur?" Apophis demanded as Erik's breathing became faster, and water formed in his eyes. Showing no compassion, Apophis poured rubbing alcohol on the open wounds.

Erik cried out in a voice raw with pain.

"Where will the landings occur?" Apophis lowered his dagger and pulled out his Lugar, pistol-whipping Erik several times.

With each strike, pain branched across his skull like lightning. Blood trickled from his lips. Apophis placed the Lugar under Erik's chin.

Erik chuckled. "Under the chin's perfect. Pull the trigger."

Apophis hid his frustration. "I can put one in your knee. And the bullet may pierce through your kneecap, and your pain cannot be measured." Apophis stared at Erik as he grabbed something known as a Dutch Scratching Knotted Rope. It was a rope with a large knot at the end.

A sickening wave of terror welled up in Erik's belly as his eyes focused on the knot. Even though he never experienced the rope, he was aware it was the most sinister torture device and any man's wildest fear.

"Erik, this simple thing will cause more pain than you can possibly endure."

Erik felt nauseating spurts of adrenaline course through his veins as his stare became catatonic. Apophis's eyes narrowed, and there was no expression on his slender face. His lack of expression revealed he was unconcerned with how much pain he would cause.

"Once I start, the immediate agony of the pain and the knowledge that it will never end will drive you to madness." A wicked grin appeared on Apophis's face. "Whether you have some pain or more pain depends on the information you provide." He spun the rope. "Know that if you do not give the information, there will be nothing left of your manhood." He leaned forward with a faint trace of impatience. "The only question remains: will you give me the information on time?"

He analyzed Erik carefully, almost caressingly, with his eyes. Then, without hesitation, his wrists sprang suddenly upwards, and the knotted rope soared toward its target. Erik's whole body arched in an involuntary spasm as pain exploded from his genitals.

Erik's chest tightened as if all the oxygen from his lungs was taken. He hyperventilated as he tried to breathe through the pain. His face contracted in agony as he let out an anguished scream. His head flew back with a jerk, showing the taut sinews of his neck as his veins popped out. Erik's muscles tightened and formed knots all over his body as his toes and fingers clenched, like an eagle's talons, until they were white. He got his breathing under control as his body, drenched in sweat, started to relax from the first blow. He slowly lifted his head and stared at Apophis as he uttered a deep groan.

Apophis stared into Erik's eyes. "You see," he said with an apathetic look. "It is up to you if you want this to continue." Apophis, without mercy or remorse, struck again. "Where will the landings occur?" He struck again.

Again, all the air was knocked out of Erik. As he cringed, tears of pain formed in his eyes as he let out an ear-splitting, gut-wrenching scream.

Apophis noticed Erik was disoriented from the pain, so he reached for a bottle and opened it. "You seem to enjoy these experiences." He poured more rubbing alcohol on Erik's open wounds. "The landings?" Pain engulfed his chest as it continued to spread throughout his body. "The landings?" He poured the remaining rubbing alcohol.

Erik grunted as his eyes turned into rage.

Apophis grabbed salt, from a bag and pressed it into Erik's wounds like tiny shards of glass.

Erik arched his back, holding his breath to suppress another scream as pain exploded across his body again.

"The landings?"

Erik knew there was no rescue coming for him. He started to think there was also no possibility of escape.

Apophis settled himself in a chair opposite Erik and poured

some water into a glass. "Erik." He took a sip of water. "Don't underestimate me. I will get what I need. I know you know more than you speak. I notice more than you realize." He put his glass of water down as he stood up. "Now, let us get down to business, although I am sure you would like this to end and are thinking of an amusing and cautionary tale to tell me."

He suddenly dropped his tongue-in-cheek talk and looked at Erik sharply and venomously as he picked up the rope and spun it again. Apophis's wrist jerked, driving the knot into Erik's testicles, sending his whole body into involuntary contortions. He waited until Erik's tortured body relaxed and his eyes fully opened and stuck him again. "I should explain," Apophis said. "I am not trying to kill you, but I intend to continue attacking the sensitive parts of your body until you answer my question. Once I get what I need, we can be finished with this unfortunate mess you have gotten yourself into." Apophis jerked his wrist ever so slightly.

"Wait," Erik mumbled as he looked at Apophis. "I will tell you what I know."

Apophis crossed his arms against his chest.

"Pas de Calais."

Apophis grabbed Erik's chin firmly so he could look into his eyes. "What did you say?"

"Pas de Calais."

"What about Pas de Calais?" He studied Erik's body language. "The landings?"

Erik nodded as he mumbled, "You want to know the code names of our beach sectors?"

Apophis nodded as he prepared to make mental notes.

"Utah, Omaha, Gold, Juno and Sword."

He grinned inwardly, nodded, and was clearly pleased that the information Erik was providing was accurate from his sources. He motioned Erik to continue.

"Do you want to know about the disposition of troops in the various sectors?"

Apophis gestured for him to continue.

"Utah was the US 31st Corps with the US 14th Division making an initial assault. Omaha was the US 33rd Corps with the US 17th and 22nd divisions. Gold was assigned to the US 55th and 59th divisions, with the US 50th making the landing at Juno. And Sword, the US 130th."

Apophis rubbed his chin while looking at Erik with menacing eyes. "I see. I'm just curious. Why are you telling me this now? Of course, the Abwehr can confirm everything you are saying."

Erik was coping with the pain, but it would not be the last of it. Apophis who brought Erik to the brink of death, where he could still answer his questions despite suffering from unimaginable pain.

"You are telling the truth now, hmm?" Apophis asked, and Erik nodded. However, Apophis knew to stay quiet and not utter a single word or gesture. He stared at Erik. Based on Apophis's past experience, he knew he would make the person he was interrogating question or second-guess their answer. He also presumed Erik was familiar with this technique, as well. Apophis stood up and nodded, exuding confidence and power. "You know I am a medical doctor, and I can ease your pain." He headed to a small table and made sure Erik saw the morphine there as he continued in a warm voice. "I see you noticed what's on the table, and I can assure you I am a man of my word. Give me what I need, and the pain will stop." He pivoted to face Erik. "There is a good chance confusion, anger, and fear consume you."

He placed his hand on bundles of neatly stacked manila folders. Then, he grabbed a newspaper and started reading, occasionally glancing at Erik. "Would you kindly ponder this question: What am I going to do next?" He grinned menacingly. "After all,

I do know something." He continued reading and positioned the newspaper so Erik could see the wording was in English, then strolled toward Erik. "You can see that I know all about your invasion."

He folded the newspaper and meticulously creased it so only the headline was showing and glanced over it with his cold, blue, calculating eyes. "I have to admit, the *New York Times* does an amazing job of reporting the news."

Erik lifted his battered and bruised face, taking on dark shades of blue, purple, and black from the beatings.

"If you don't believe me, read it yourself."

Erik struggled to open his eyes, which felt like glue held them down because of the lack of sleep. The headline read: *ALLIED ARMIES FAIL TO LAND IN FRANCE ON THE NORMANDY COAST; GREAT LOSS OF LIFE; EISENHOWER STEPS DOWN.*

Erik shook his head, gave a slight grin, and chuckled. "There must have been a moment when you thought this would work." He gave the newspaper a once-over and chuckled more. "The font is the wrong size. Because of being in the SS, somehow you missed it."

Erik wasn't sure what day it was; however, he knew that Apophis's job was to listen to Erik's information. Several methods can obtain information, such as observing for any gaps in his voice or inflections. In either case, Apophis would know if Erik were lying. However, Erik knew he could call the newspaper a bluff. Even though the SS had no way of proving the font size was off, it would make them question it. This would give him a few more hours to plan his escape. On the other hand, what if the newspaper was real? There was only one way to find out, and that was to test the waters.

"I believe you are wrong, general." Apophis paused a moment

before studying Erik out of the corner of his eye with his arms crossed. "How would you know so much about this paper's type-setting?"

"I read it all the time, and my father worked for them." Erik glanced up again. "You ever lived in America, you ignorant SS fuck?"

"I can see in your eyes that our time together has had little effect on you. However…" Apophis pulled a photograph from his pocket. "Not bad, Erik. You have good taste." Apophis looked at Erik as he turned the photograph around, then asked, "How much younger is she?" He looked down at Erik with a mischievous grin rife with evil, but Erik showed no reaction to his question. "Your wife," Apophis stated. "It's nice to see your wife lives in London. I know that from the background. You should know I have people in London, and they will find her, as I found you."

Erik let out an enormous sigh.

"Looks like I found the thing that makes you tick." He narrowed his eyes as he leaned forward. "It's going to drive you crazy, not knowing what we will do to her." Apophis could see the hate swelling in Erik. "Don't worry, I promise they won't do anything until she is here, so that you can hear her screaming." He crossed his arms. "Your wife is going to moan like a whore when we ravage her again, and again, and again, until it drives you crazy. Then, I will personally gut her like a fish. I will make Jack the Ripper look like an amateur."

Erik's eyes were filled with rage as Apophis continued.

"The darkness I possess will consume you and everything you possess, and I will take everything away from you." Apophis relished in the moment, realizing he was getting to Erik. "All your anger and hatred won't save her, and no one can save you." Apophis got so close that Erik could smell his breath and see his stained teeth. "I will make sure the information you gave me is correct."

Erik took a deep breath and said as he exhaled, "I have an absolute duty to kill you. I don't know how yet but give me time."

Apophis stood upright and smiled. "The next time we meet will be the first day of the rest of your life."

CHAPTER 23

THE SECRET RIDDLE OF WHERE

"All warfare is based on deception. Hence, when we are able to attack, we must seem unable; when using our forces, we must appear inactive; when we are near, we must make the enemy believe we are far away; when far away, we must make him believe we are near."

— Sun Tzu, *The Art of War*

Apophis headed to his encryption team that handles communication with the Royal Botanical Garden Society. Once there, he ordered them to send an urgent message.

```
exxpe sojyt hqvna lqcvz apfav vzefi kotrj oeeus
pyfvl aafap tupog sviks jhqkz tytnc xxpsp
pqbal kmref hygox qmxao jgpol pmabo tmksy yt-
rxe glzrg mfyer gwsqs mcdrg ukcqo xgtmh lfuvl
jvgnw leaib cosbf icdzx wxjjd viivl qxpsf kq-
taf ntffi gqwcn thyr
```

Each letter of the message was typed in the ciphertext, and the letters that were lit were the decoded letters. What made it an amazing machine was inside the box. The system was built around three physical rotors. As the operator types each letter, it outputs it as a different letter. First, the letter passes through a series of three rotors. The first rotor clicked and turned through all twenty-six positions until it reached one position, thus changing the output even if the second letter is the same as the first one. The second rotor did the same as the first, and when it had completed its full rotation, the third repeated the process. Once that process was done, it bounced off a reflector at the end, then passed back through all three rotors in the other direction. Finally, the board lit up to show the encrypted output. Because of that, the Enigma machine had over seventeen thousand different combinations before the encryption process repeated itself, making all communication of commercial, diplomatic, and other branches of the German military, even the SS, secure.

The message read: *A simple exercise in logistics. Find Jamie Foge. Lives in or near Claridge's in London. Brunette, brown eyes, approximately five feet four inches, petite, late twenties. Advise the excavation team to locate the flower and deliver it within twenty-four hours. Most critical.*

Apophis ordered the operator to inform him as soon as he received any reports and to update him as to their progress. Apophis was not a patient man, so the operator gave a quick nod and replied, "Jawohl."

Immediately following, Apophis headed down a hallway and barged into the office of Colonel Wilhelm Meyer-Detring, Rundstedt's Chief Intelligence Officer, who was talking to Lieutenant Colonel Hellmuth Meyers, the Fifteenth Army's intelligence officer, who headed up the only counterintelligence team on the invasion front. He tossed the newspaper on his desk.

"The font is wrong. He knew the paper was a fake." Apophis stated in a voice that chilled the air.

"I don't see that as our problem." Wilhelm stood up and replied with a confident, arrogant expression as he pointed to the newspaper. "Your people did that. You need to address that to them."

Apophis turned to stare into Hellmuth's fatigued and sleep-deprived eyes, who had not had a good night's sleep since June first. "I have some information he provided. Can you verify?"

Hellmuth nodded. "Do you still believe the allies will land in Normandy?"

Apophis nodded as he handed over his notes from the interrogation.

Hellmuth shook his head in disbelief. "I have a thirty-man radio interception crew who works around the clock." He emphasized each word clearly. He continued explaining that his men were using delicate radio equipment to listen to allied communication. What made his team effective at their job was each man was an expert who spoke three languages fluently. In addition, there was hardly a word or Morse code from allied sources they did not hear, and the equipment his team used was so sensitive that they could even pick up calls from radio transmitters in military jeeps in England, more than a hundred miles away.

Hellmuth looked over Apophis's notes and, once he spotted something of interest, he placed the paper on the desk. "We heard American and British MPs chatting with one another by radio as they directed troop convoys for the US 55th and 59th divisions, having more tanks sent to the coast." He pointed at Apophis to get his point across. "I can assure you; my men are compiling a list of the various divisions stationed in England. Our best troops will await them when they land at Pas de Calais."

Wilhelm faced Apophis. He remained unconvinced and terse. "What makes you so sure the landings are going to be at Normandy?"

Apophis walked to a map and dragged his finger from the English coastline to Pas de Calais. "Everyone believes that this is where the Allies will cross because it is the nearest to mainland Europe." He repositioned himself on the other side of the map. "If you look here," Apophis pointed to Cherbourg, "this is a large port the Allies could use, and it is directly across the channel from the principal ports of southern England: Portsmouth and Southampton."

Then, he pointed at Normandy. "If the Allies land here, it will be easier to land tanks, equipment, and supplies. Within days or weeks, they could take Cherbourg, allowing Allied forces to flow freely into France."

Then he pointed to several areas near the Normandy coast. "The last couple of days, allied bombers have struck railways and bridges in northern France, which would slow the flow of our forces moving to react to a landing in Normandy."

Hellmuth scoffed. "I have time every day reading through piles of reports. I am always on the lookout for the suspicious, the unusual, and even the unbelievable." He walked to the map and pointed at Normandy. "I can assure you, if we had an inkling the landings would be there, I would be the first to know."

He picked up a cable and handed it to Apophis. "Yesterday, my men picked up something unbelievable. This message was a high-speed press cable." He pointed at the wording. It read: *URGENT PRESS ASSOCIATED NYK FLASH EISENHOWER'S HQ ANNOUNCES ALLIED LANDINGS IN FRANCE.*

Apophis looked dumbfounded.

Hellmuth continued. "The message was false for two reasons. Do you remember Admiral Wilhelm Canaris? He was chief of German intelligence."

Apophis nodded. "Canaris warned in January that the Allies would broadcast hundreds of messages to the underground in the months preceding the attack. Also, he told me the details of a two-part signal which he said the Allies would use to alert the underground prior to the invasion. First, there is a complete absence of activity along the invasion front and on the English Channel, which would precede any kind of attack. Additionally, with the Allies sending so many messages, we know the majority of them are fake, intentionally meant to mislead us and create confusion on our part."

Wilhelm added, "Pas de Calais bridges and railroads are being bombed just like Normandy. I believe, and so does he," he motioned to Hellmuth, "the Allies are trying to mislead and confuse us."

There was a pounding on the door, followed by a sergeant bursting into the office and staring at Hellmuth. "Sir, the first part of the message is here."

Hellmuth's eyes grew wide. "Very good, Sergeant Reichling. Continue."

"The long sobs of the violins of autumn." The sergeant paused for a moment, then repeated the message.

"What does that mean?" Apophis demanded.

Hellmuth explained it was the first line of *"Song of Autumn"* by the nineteenth-century French poet Paul Verlaine. He added that Admiral Canaris's information was scheduled to be transmitted on the first or fifteenth of the past two months. It was the first half of a message announcing the Anglo-American invasion. However, it was odd that it was being sent on the fourth of June. The second part of the message would confirm the date and time of the invasion, but they would have to wait for that.

Upon hearing the sergeant's report, Wilhelm dismissed Hellmuth with a wave of his hand. After that, he addressed Apophis with a stern, impersonal voice and pointed at him to get his point across. "Find out where in the hell the Anglo-American invasion will be. Confirm it, report directly to me, and then you can do whatever you want to the general."

Apophis clicked his heels, made an about-face, and left.

Wilhelm headed to the main conference room behind a guarded set of double doors. They opened to a vast, open room adjoining smaller spaces bustling with activity. In them, individuals sorted through files, answered telephones, and analyzed Teletype messages. Several members of the German High Command of Western Europe analyzed a large map of the northern European coast and southern England, complete with both Allied and Axis military assets, on a long table.

Wilhelm approached the table where Colonel Professor Walter Stobe, the Luftwaffe's chief meteorologist, was about to begin his briefing. Also in the room were Field Marshal Von Rundstedt, Commander-in-Chief West, responsible for the defense of all of Western Europe, and an ambitious Field Marshal Rommel, Commander-in-Chief of Army Group B. Apophis was also there.

"Gentlemen," Stobe began, "The weather has been bad for several days, and I can promise the weather to be even worse for the next couple of days." Rundstedt and Rommel looked for further explanation. "I'm predicting increasing cloudiness, high winds, and rain."

Rundstedt dismissed Stobe and stared at Apophis, then said in a high, authoritative, and impatient tone. "What did you find out, Herr Colonel?"

Apophis took a deep breath. He leaned forward as he made eye contact with the field marshals. "The fake newspaper didn't work, but rest assured, I got what I needed to find out about the landings."

Rundstedt squinted. "I heard the SS, especially you, are capable of breaking prisoners." Rundstedt stressed his next point as he smashed his fist against the table. "We've lost precious hours unnecessarily with your questionable interrogation techniques. You were here to find out where the Anglo-American landings will be.

From now on, until we find out or I hear from you directly with proof, I will not commit any troops from the Fifteenth Army to assist the Seventh Army, which is still holding the coast of Normandy."

Apophis left without saying a word.

Rundstedt turned to Rommel. "I believe you are going to be able to see your wife on her birthday." Rommel nodded, both men exchanged salutes, and Rommel left the room. Then, Rundstedt faced Colonel Wilhelm Meyer-Detring. Their eyes locked, then they stared at the map, and again at each other. The last contact lasted only a moment, and Colonel Meyer-Detring knew exactly what Rundstedt wanted. Rundstedt had absolute confidence in Wilhelm and his team to find out where the Anglo-American landings would take place.

After Rundstedt left to return to his headquarters, Wilhelm headed to Hellmuth and his team. Reichling was firmly clapping his hands over his earphones, then he tore them off, stared at Wilhelm, and Hellmuth, and advised the message was repeating. Wilhelm asked Reichling if he had recorded the message. Reichling nodded. At that moment, Wilhelm grabbed the headset, and as he listened, his eyes enlarged immediately on hearing the recording of the first line from Verlaine. He motioned Hellmuth to get Major General Rudolf Hofmann, Fifteenth Army's chief of staff, on the phone and advise him about the message.

Hellmuth picked up the receiver and asked the operator to connect him to Major General Rudolf Hofmann as Wilhelm continued to listen. A few minutes later, the call was connected.

"This is Hofmann."

"Herr General, this is Lieutenant Colonel Hellmuth Meyer. I know Field Marshal Rundstedt is not there, but you need to advise him about something that is going to happen."

"Are you absolutely sure?" Hofmann replied in a hesitant tone.

"Yes, Herr General, we recorded it," Meyer replied.

"I will take care of it, Herr Colonel. Keep me informed."

Immediately following, Hofmann sounded the alarm to alert the whole of the Fifteenth Army. Meyer, meanwhile, sent the message by Teletype to Oberkommando der Wehrmacht, High Command of the Armed Forces. At OKW, the message was delivered to Colonel General Alfred Jodl, Chief of Operations. He had been getting these same messages ever since June 1. Jodl thought Rommel's headquarters had issued the order and that Rommel must have known about the message, but from his own estimate of Anglo-American landings and intentions. He did not order an alert. He assumed Rundstedt would do that once he came back to his headquarters. Along the invasion coast, only one army was on readiness: the Fifteenth. He left the message, that remained on his desk, and went to bed.

Colonel Wilhelm Meyer-Detring and Lieutenant Colonel Hellmuth Meyer sat quietly, as there was nothing they could do but wait for the last half of the vital alert.

CHAPTER 24

MADNESS 3: FLESH, BLOOD, BONE, AND THOUGHTS

"Things we lose have a way of coming back to us in the end, if not always in the way we expect."
— Luna Lovegood, *Harry Potter and the Order of the Phoenix*

Erik lay bleeding on the floor in a grotesque position, with his body twisted into a bloody fetal position. A large swelling persisted over his eyes, and his face was black, with thick blisters and thick, open wounds that had ripped into pieces, exposing raw meat beneath. His inflamed, cracked lips oozed blood mixed with saliva from the corners of his mouth to form a puddle. His body felt like every muscle had been twisted and pulled in ways he did not understand. He stiffened in apprehension every time his groin convulsed with pain. As he tried to recover and find some way to manage his pain, he cringed every time he moved because he feared he would hurt himself even more.

He recalled what he had learned at the farm. *Do not think about the pain.* Rusch said in his last statement about the pain he and others might experience, "You adjust for it. You make minor adjustments." Those words helped little, but he still took shallow breaths and tried to clear his mind.

What made things worse, he couldn't recall how long the beating had gone on. The situation far exceeded any nightmare that he could ever have contemplated. However, the Germans did not know where the D-Day landings were going to take place. That offered him some comfort. However, he wasn't sure if it was June 6 yet or how close it was. He still had to hold out until after the invasion.

Erik knew he would likely die in that cell, or perhaps during the next torture session. When he volunteered to go back in time, he knew he would have to give up a lot of things and make sacrifices in order to accomplish his task. The things he had seen and experienced filled his mind, leaving him unable to find peace within himself, especially since Jamie was not there to comfort him. When Erik traveled back in time, he felt as if he were putting himself on an unreversible journey. At that point, he is left with his unwillingness to give up, his eagerness to fight to preserve history, his knowledge of history, and his anger and stubbornness.

Erik never yearned to become a hero fighting against those who sought to change history to suit their own interests or benefit. Occasionally, Erik looked down at his feet as if there was no moral ground beneath him, only his integrity. As a CIA paramilitary operations officer, he uses his skills and tools to preserve history and defeat those who want to change it. He knew there was always a chance he wouldn't see another day. In order for Erik to achieve his goal of preserving history, what sacrifices would he make? His life.

Erik took a deep breath and slowly exhaled to clear his mind. *Jamie,* he thought, *they say I should feel noble and righteous for fighting to preserve history, but I don't. I feel small, like a pawn on a chessboard that is the size of a football field. Sometimes, I feel selfish because I want to do more, but I can't. I can't erase the physical and mental anguish. I ask myself, why don't I go back and save you? What kind* of God is making me go through these hellish journeys? It feels like an unpredictable card game, never knowing what the rules are. What I feel is like being hit with a pick axe in my soul. I try to say it will pass, but it's bullshit.

He tried to tell himself not to get angry or take it personally. He tried to let it go. It was killing him. He thinks, *fuck that*. The only positive thing left in Erik is Jamie. He mumbled the words to himself, "I love you. I was wrong. This time, I won't survive. I hope you can forgive me. I will see you soon."

Erik was getting colder and clammy. He was trying to keep warm in any way possible and knew he was probably in shock. As a result of being tortured for the past few days, his vision was blurred, his sense of smell lacking, and his body was physically drained. It was as if he were drifting into a dream state.

When he opened his eyes, he was surprised to see Jamie standing quietly beside him in the middle of the room. He firmly believed it was a mental illusion caused by lack of sleep. He turned away and closed his eyes. In his ear, he could hear a sweet, loving voice whispering something to him. It would not give up and kept calling his name, but what was the point of it? He had been lucky to remember his name. He was lucky to remember hers. He rolled over and raised his head to stare at her.

"Jamie?" Erik struggled to utter as his eyes tried to focus. "Jamie?" He wasn't sure if she was real or a hallucination. Did his mind conjure her to escape the unbearable agony he was experiencing? She looked at him with warm eyes and a soft smile that could melt a heart of ice, with tears trickling down her cheeks.

She kneeled beside him, gently stroking his head and reassuring him that everything would be alright. Her smile faded to concern, then bewilderment, as if she couldn't comprehend how a person could be so evil as to treat Erik in such a way. "You look awful. How can someone be so cruel and twisted?"

Erik looked into her eyes. "I don't think I can endure much longer. I'm tired, and I can tell my mind is cracking." Erik tried to sit upright, exposing his blackened, blood-encrusted chest. Blood dripped from his mouth. Jamie pressed her hand over her mouth and gasped for breath. "You can see the scars on my body, but there are more on the inside." Erik paused for a moment before continuing. As he leaned against a wall to support, he blurted out, "I'm so tired, Jamie. I'm not sure if there is anything left of me."

"Erik, don't give up hope. You have inner strength and tenacity in every step you take." She moved closer. "Believe in yourself, because I believe in you."

"I don't know if I can." Erik tilted his head back. "I can't see straight and don't know how long I've been here. When they torture me, it feels like a shotgun blast tearing me to pieces. With every method they use, I wonder if I can continue."

Unbeknownst to Erik, the SS were watching and listening to him. There were microphones in his cell. Apophis was experimenting with a newly devised form of torture.

"Herr Colonel, it appears he is talking to himself."

"It's because of a lack of sleep," Apophis explained. "He will break and tell me what I need."

Apophis sat at a table with a machine covered in switches and lighted buttons, and in the center was a huge gauge. The gauge was divided into colored sections ranging from green to yellow, orange, then red. Numbers ran along the gauge in increments of ten, ranging from zero to one hundred and fifty. A single word was displayed below the gauge, *DEZIBELPEGE*—decibel level. The needle climbed as Apophis slowly turned a dial. Ten, twenty...

Erik again took a deep breath as he stared at Jamie. "I miss you." He rubbed his eyes with the palms of his hands, then ran his fingers through his hair. "I'm ashamed for you to see me like this."

"Erik, I am not ashamed. What makes you amazing is that it surprises everyone, including me, when the world comes crashing down. You hop right back up to fix it." She gets in his face. "I want to see you win."

As Apophis turned the gauge, he was convinced he was making progress. Thirty, forty, fifty, sixty...

"You believed me?" Erik asked.

She nodded.

"Outside these walls is an SS colonel who is intent on getting information from me by torturing me and making me wish I was dead. No one knows where I am. I've been brought here to rot or die."

As the needle on the gauge continued to move, the pain continued to rise. Seventy, eighty, ninety...

A high-pitched squeal assaulted Erik's ears. He snapped his head back, but he felt paralyzed. The pain forced his eyelids open, his heart pounded in his chest, and his blood rushed through his veins. Clinging to the wall, he pushed himself up. "Listen to me," Erik continued, focusing on his wife's face. "Darling, I love you still, even though we have parted. You are my one and only love who gave me strength when I needed it most." Tears welled up in his eyes. "I would give everything just to have you back again."

Apophis's scowl deepened as he continued to turn the knob, glaring at Erik as the stubborn American continued to resist. One hundred, one hundred and ten, one hundred and twenty...

Erik cringed from the pain in his ears. His head spun and ached, and his vision blurred. Jamie's words buttressed his confidence and strength. It was as if the words she spoke were like oxygen that filled his lungs as he focused on them. "Now, it's my turn to give back that power and strength that is within you still, only hidden, buried deep within. You are my love. Now, I awaken our power together that denies any weakness or doubt inside of you."

The needle rose through the numbers and colors. Long past the green, beyond the yellow, and even leaving orange behind. Into the red it rose. One hundred and thirty, one hundred and forty, and finally the knob clicked and would turn no further, despite Apophis's urging, as the needle hovered over one hundred and fifty.

Erik's screams echoed through the cell, amplified by the stone walls. His eyes transformed from weak and beaten to burning with irrational rage.

"You're my knight and are unstoppable, now, always, and forevermore."

As Jamie faded into the blackness, Erik's expression changed from drawn, wretched, and ready to surrender into one filled with determination to fight for what he believes in and shoulder the weight of the world. An unseen power took control of Erik, and he yelled in defiance at those who were trying to break him.

CHAPTER 25

LATE NIGHT WITH HEADPHONES ON AS DARKNESS FADES

"The whole secret lies in confusing the enemy, so that he cannot fathom our real intent."

— Sun Tzu, *The Art of War*

JUNE 6, 1944, 12:30 AM

An oscillating fan's motor hummed, permeating the damp, dark environment of the office. A single light shone on the desk, breaking the darkness, as the blades of the fan struggled to push air through the metal guard. The light diffused around classified documents, photographs of the ports and areas around Kent and Dover, draft cables, and memoranda spread across the desk. Apophis rubbed his chin as he read the last communique the Royal Botanical Garden Society had sent to the encryption team.

```
TO LEAD HORTICULTURIST: EXCAVATION TEAM HAS
NOT FOUND THE FLOWER YOU REQUESTED. STILL NEED
TIME.
```

A gentle knock on his office door shifted his focus. He raised his eyes from the communique, examining every part of the man's uniform. He wore polished jackboots, crisp, dry-cleaned black slacks, and a belt buckle of polished silver embossed with a large eagle, wings outstretched, clutching a wreathed swastika. A ribbed border with a stylized pattern surrounded this, and below was a banner with the words *Meine Ehre heißt Treue*—My honor is my loyalty. On the upper right sleeve of the uniform jacket was a single chevron, a symbol of his old fighter status. As one of the old fighters, he was a member of the Nazi party, as they joined the SS in January of 1933. An additional distinguishing feature of this individual's uniform was the ribbon of the blood order that was affixed to the buttonhole of his right breast pocket. The highly exclusive Nazi medal was awarded to those who took part in the 1923 Beer Hall Putsch.

On the individual's left breast pocket hung a golden Nazi party badge. In addition, he wore a Wing Badge, which combined a pilot's observation badge in gold and an eagle filled with diamonds with its talons holding a swastika. Hermann Göring must have given it to him.

Apophis realized who stood in front of him in their immaculate black SS uniform: Reichsführer Heinrich Himmler. In response, Apophis stood at attention and saluted, which Himmler returned in kind.

"Take your seat, Herr Colonel," Himmler said, gesturing to the chair behind Apophis. The man's cold, apathetic blue eyes peered through gold-rimmed, circular glasses sitting atop the sharp tip of his nose. He gave a half-sardonic smile which conveyed he was superior to anyone who stood in front of him.

"I heard this general didn't fall for your forgery of the *New York Times*, and he is proving resilient to torture." Apophis nodded as Himmler pulled out a glass vial containing Mescaline on the desk. "Bypass what you are doing and use this." He pushed a vial toward Apophis.

"I have considered that. But the side effects—"

"There's nothing to consider! Use it," Himmler demanded.

"We must measure what we might gain by what we might lose."

"You should have extracted the information two days ago." Despite this, Himmler looked at him to explain further.

"My usual methods failed, which is a first. I must break him another way."

"We are wasting time. Time, Apophis, is something of which you have little."

"Herr Reichsführer, in two hours, my encryption team will give me an update from the Royal Botanical Garden Society."

"Colonel Adelram, you will not wait for that message. Proceed with the use of Mescaline. That's an order."

"Yes, sir. Herr Reichsführer, before you leave, may I show you something?" Apophis placed a photograph in front of Himmler.

He picked up the photo, gave it little more than a disinterested glance, then tossed it back on the desk. "What is it?"

"That's the general's wife. If you look closely, you will see Big Ben in the background."

"And?"

"Herr Reichsführer, do you realize what this means? It means he was staying at Claridge's, which is within walking distance of Big Ben. I cannot break his body, but I have the opportunity to break his morale and destroy his will to fight. It's within my reach. That is why you must permit me to wait for my update. Once I have her, he will tell me everything we need to know about where the Anglo-American landings will take place, and then I will kill them both."

Himmler looked at his watch. "You have until zero three hundred hours. That is all." The reichsführer then stood.

Apophis stood at attention and saluted. Himmler returned the salute before leaving. The colonel stormed out of his office and to his encryption team, demanding an update from the Royal Botanical Garden Society on the situation. "Bring any message to me as soon as you hear from them so I can act on it immediately." He then ordered for the interrogation room to be set up and for Erik to be brought there in fifteen minutes.

RENNES, FRANCE, 1:00 AM

General Erich Marcks and his intelligence officer, Major Friedrich Hayn, stood and walked around a long, sturdy wooden table with war maps spread out across it. Marcks removed his spectacles and rubbed his eyes as he studied the latest map that was brought out.

"Herr General, it looks like you are preparing for a game of Kriegsspiel[2] of the invasion of Normandy as though it were a real battle instead of merely a theoretical," Hayn stated.

Marcks nodded in agreement. He had heard of Apophis and, through rumors, what he was doing. Even though he was not fond of the SS, both Marcks and Apophis agreed the invasion would be at Normandy. An enlisted man handed a communique to Hayn. Looking up from the maps, Marcks asked. "Anything important?"

Reading from the document, Hayn replied, "Communications reports difficulty in reaching our forward posts."

As he strolled around the table, Marcks said, "It is probably the French Underground again." He rolled his eyes because that was becoming a weekly occurrence.

Hayn held up a hand and shook his head in disbelief. "There are reports of some sort of rubber dummies having been parachuted."

------

2. A genre of wargaming developed by the Prussian Army in the 19th century to teach battlefield tactics to officers. Also, used during WW2 with German officers

There was a look of puzzlement on Marcks' face as Hayne pointed at the map and explained what was going on. "Reports say these rubber dummies dropped near the base of the Cotentin Peninsula." He circled his finger around the area. "And here, and here." He pointed to the area around the River Dives and the area southwest of Caen. Finally, he pointed at Yvetot.

Marcks rubbed his chin as he studied the map. After a moment or two, his eyes widened as if a lightbulb had gone off in his head, and he was quick to realize what could be going on. He snapped his head toward Hayne. "We can expect commando raids and other diversionary tactics."

In the midst of their discussion, the phone broke the silence. On the second ring, Marcks picked up the phone. The blood appeared to have left his face as his eyes grew larger and his body stiffened. He snapped his fingers at Hayn to pick up the extension phone. The voice Hayn heard was one he recognized. It was the commander of the 716th Division, Major General Wilhelm Richter, who was in charge of ensuring that the French coastline was protected in the event of an allied amphibious invasion. The sector was bordered on the west by Bayeux, where the 352nd Infantry Division had been located since May 1944, and on the east by Caen.

"Parachutists have landed east of the Orne," Richter advised Marcks. Marcks stepped closer to the map table as Richter continued. "Also, in the areas around Breville and Ranville along the northern fringe of the Bavent Forest."

Marcks hung up the receiver as he addressed Hayn. "I do not like this idea of dummy parachutists, because we did the same thing." He was referring to when the Germans used the same tactic during their paratrooper drops in the Netherlands in 1940. He called for his orderly, an enlisted soldier that was assigned to perform various chores for Marcks. "Find Colonel Apophis Adelram."

"Who's Colonel Apophis Adelram?"

"He is with the SS."

Hayn mouthed the *SS*, unable to hide his fear as his eyes widened.

Marcks nodded as he continued. "I heard he's interrogating prisoners, and he's trying to find out where the landings will take place."

"It might be unwise to draw the attention of the SS," Hayn said.

"I agree, but he and I agree that the invasion will take place at the Normandy beaches." He studied the map again. "If I can advise him of what's going on, it might help him get the information we need, and I can prove we are correct."

"Where is he, Herr General?"

Marcks shook his head. "It is uncertain because of what he is doing. Since this was the first official report of an allied attack to reach a major headquarters, I will have proof when I go to Field Marshal Von Rundstedt if Colonel Adelram obtained information that the invasion will be at Normandy." Marcks was approached by the orderly, who informed him that Colonel Adelram was on the phone for him.

There was a crackling of static as a voice fought to come over. "Repeat, please."

"I am trying to reach Colonel Adelram, this is General Marcks," Marcks' static-riddled voice demanded.

"Colonel Adelram cannot come to the phone, sir." More crackling of static. "I can deliver a message for you, Herr General."

At that moment, an enlisted man handed another communique to Hayn. It was from the German Freya radar system site[3] at Bruneval, a coastal village near Le Havre, France. This had a maximum range of only ninety-nine miles. "They have what seems

---

3. Freya operated in the band from 8.2 to 7.5 feet which had 120 to 130 megahertz. The pulse width of the Freya was three microseconds. The radar operators peaked power output to 15 to 20 kilowatts, and a pulse repetition frequency of 500 megahertz.

to appear to be a large fleet approaching Pas de Calais[4]," Hayn said, then immediately handed the message over to Marcks, who skimmed it as he waited.

"Tell Colonel Adelram that dummy paratroopers are landing in the Normandy area, and the Freya radar system site at Bruneval has picked up a large fleet approaching Pas de Calais." The line appeared to go dead as Marcks repeatedly shouted to get someone's attention.

Then, the connection was clear. "Herr General, repeat, please."

"This is General Marcks. Tell Colonel Adelram that dummy paratroopers are landing in the Normandy area and the Freya radar system site at Bruneval has picked up a large fleet approaching Pas de Calais."

"Herr General, is that all?

"Tell Colonel Adelram to contact me at once."

Marcks then turned to Hayn and asked him to contact Major General Max Pemsel, chief of staff of the Seventh Army, about the situation. Hayn gestured to Marcks to let him know Pemsel was on the phone a few moments later. Marcks told him about the rubber dummies, saying he thought that it was a diversion, and about the fleet picked up by the radar station. Pemsel agreed, and he said he would call Marcks back as soon as possible once he learned more about the situation.

LE MANS, FRANCE, 2:15 AM

Pemsel demanded that Von Rundstedt take his call, but his

---

4. Allied aircraft flying toward Pas de Calais dropped clouds of aluminum strips to give false radar readings that made it appear a large fleet was approaching Pas de Calais.

communications staff were unable to reach him, surmising the main lines had been cut or the telephone poles knocked down. Pemsel put the Seventh on Alarm Struffe II, the highest state of readiness, taking no chances with the situation. His staff were able to contact and awaken the commander of the Seventh Division, Colonel General Friedrich Dollmann, who had been sleeping for some time.

Pemsel accepted the telephone receiver and said, "Herr General, I believe this is the beginning of the invasion."

Dollmann agreed and advised him he would call Von Rundstedt to brief him on the situation.

Next, Pemsel contacted Rommel's chief of staff at Army Group B, Lieutenant General Dr. Hans Speidel, to brief him on what was going on. By then, it was 2:35 AM.

TOURCOING, FRANCE, 2:50 AM

As the Fifteenth Army headquarters was busy with in-coming reports about paratroopers in Normandy, Colonel General Hans von Salmuth, commanding the 2nd Army based in the Pas de Calais region, was preparing for an Allied invasion. Not long after, he took command of the 15th Army, which was eighteen divisions strong and defended the French coast from Le Havre northeastwards to the estuary of the Schelde River, near the Belgian border. All the while, he was trying to obtain first-hand information.

A report was sent to him by the Freya radar system at Bruneval, indicating that a large fleet was approaching Pas de Calais. It had not been confirmed visually. As a result, he did nothing at all. When he heard that there was fighting around Caen, he immediately called Lieutenant General Josef Reichert, who was in command of the 711th Infantry Division, which had moved to Normandy to defend the coast against any attempts by the Allies to land.

"Reichert, what the devil is going on down there?" He demanded.

Reichert seemed stressed. "Herr General, if you'll permit me, I'll let you hear for yourself." There was a moment of silence, then Von Salmuth heard orders being barked and bursts of clattering machine gun fire.

"Thank you, Reichert. Keep me informed." After hanging up the phone, Von Salmuth dialed Army Group B, Rommel's headquarters. Vice-Admiral Friedrich Ruge, who was Rommel's naval aide, was connected with Von Salmuth. "Admiral Ruge, this is Colonel General Hans von Salmuth. I just got off the phone with Lieutenant General Josef Reichert. The 711th Infantry Division is under attack. Is this the invasion?"

"Herr, General," Admiral Ruge said, accompanied by the sound of shuffling papers, "There have been reports coming in of airborne troops. They were only dolls disguised as paratroopers."

LE MANS, FRANCE, 3:00 AM

Taking a deep breath, Major General Pemsel looked at his watch for the first time in several days, then looked desperately at the map of Normandy and assessed the growing number of red spots sprouting from it. He turned to one of his staff members and said, "They would not drop dummies unless it was diverting our attention from something else."

"In this weather?" the staffer asked, gesturing to the window being buffeted by rain.

Pemsel snapped back, "In any kind of weather." Then, he turned to a junior officer and ordered, "I must get in touch with OB West and Rommel's chief of staff." The junior quickly left. Pemsel turned to his staff and stated, "From the latest reports, this is how I see it, American paratroopers have landed here." He pointed to the Cotentin Peninsula. "And British paratroopers here." He pointed to the area east of the Orne. "The invasion will be here." On the map, he drew with a pencil a line from the southern coast of England to the northern coast of Normandy. He was confident, but convincing others would be a challenge. The junior officer returned and said they were still trying to reach Von Rundstedt, but Rommel's chief of staff, Lieutenant General Dr. Hans Speidel, was on the phone.

Pemsel picked up the phone. "Speidel, both American and British paratroopers have shown up at each end of the Seventh's area, from the Cotentin Peninsula to the east of the Orne." Another junior officer handed Pemsel several reports, which he quickly read. "I'm looking at reports from naval stations at Cherbourg. Using a sound direction apparatus and some radar equipment, the stations have picked up ships maneuvering in the Bay of the Seine."

Speidel cut in before Pemsel could continue. "The affair is still locally confined."

Pemsel made a futile attempt to argue his case but was cut off.

Speidel continued. "I believe that for the time being, this is not to be considered a large operation. This is not serious enough yet to call Field Marshal Rommel. Good night, Pemsel."

Pemsel slammed the phone down as he faced his staff. "Speidel doesn't believe it's serious enough yet to call Rommel."

A junior officer advised Pemsel that Major General Blumentritt, from the OB West, was on the phone.

Pemsel picked up the phone again. "Herr General, I need to speak to Field Marshal Von Rundstedt regarding an urgent matter."

"He is on another call. What can I do?"

"American and British paratroopers have shown up at each end of the Seventh's area, from the Cotentin Peninsula to the east of the Orne. These constitute the first phase of a larger enemy action."

"Admiral Krancke's headquarters has reported that the enemy has dropped straw dummies," Blumentritt replied. "Pemsel, this is not a large-scale airborne operation."

Pemsel protested. "Sir, I'm looking at reports from naval stations at Cherbourg. They picked up ships maneuvering in the Bay of the Seine. There are even engine noises audible from out at sea."

Blumentritt picked up the reports that were given to him nearly five minutes ago. "Pemsel, I have the same reports. In addition to that, on the coast, several Kriegsmarine artillerymen spotted dark silhouettes over the horizon. They used flares to request the identification of these ships, and there was no answer. The radar listening station in Port-en-Bessin-Huppain spotted several echoes from the open sea, indicating the presence of vessels. Immediately, the 6th gunboat fleet was deployed, but we have not heard from them yet. We sent out additional patrols. They were deployed from Le Havre and Cherbourg, the 4th and 5th flotilla of torpedo boats, and the 15th patrol fleet. The 15th reported they went through a smoke curtain, possibly set up by the 6th gunboat fleet. It has appeared the Allied armada turned back after the gunboats fired their torpedoes."

Blumentritt paused for a moment before continuing. "So, Pemsel, I would not worry. The field marshal and I believe Normandy is the site of a diversion. The main landings will take place at Pas de Calais, and we will be ready for them. Pemsel, I know you are going to ask if we can move our panzers to the coast. The answer is no. Good night, Pemsel."

Pemsel placed the phone down as he faced his staff and shook his head. They all knew it was another failed attempt to convince the powers that be. In a few hours, they would know whether he was right or not.

Blumentritt hung up the phone and approached Von Rundstedt, who was standing and studying a map of France's coastline facing the English Channel. "Pemsel is convinced this is the invasion."

Field Marshal Von Rundstedt shook his head in disgust and replied in a bitter tone, "No, no, no, I do not agree with him or Rommel. If Rommel knew about this, he would break orders and move his panzers to the coast."

He pointed at the map. "Normandy is the site of a diversion. A diversion, Blumentritt!" He moved his finger to emphasize his next point. "That is not where the main landings will take place. That will come at Pas de Calais, where it was always expected."

Blumentritt said nothing as Von Rundstedt muttered to himself, "Where we always expected it." Then, the field marshal cleared his throat and addressed Blumentritt. "We can't take any chances. I want the reserve panzers moved forward." He realized he was thinking like Rommel for a second.

Blumentritt said, "But we need permission from the Führer's headquarters to move them."

Von Rundstedt nodded. "They won't dare refuse me. Call the Führer's headquarters and insist. *Insist*, Blumentritt! Insist the panzers be released to me."

Blumentritt nodded and left to call Berlin.

Von Rundstedt returned to the map and said to himself, "A landing at Normandy would be against military logic. It would be against all logic."

CHAPTER 26

METHODS 4: ALL THE WORLD IS ON YOUR SHOULDERS

"The only hope you have is to accept the fact that you're already dead. The sooner you accept that, the sooner you'll be able to function as a soldier is supposed to function: without mercy, without compassion, without remorse. All war depends upon it."
— Ronald Spiers, *Band of Brothers*

JUNE 6, 1944, 12:45 AM

Again, Erik's head was hooded as guards marched him from his cell, just as the previous five times he was tortured. Upon arriving in an unseen room, his arms were raised until they were stretched above his head, and the guards fastened handcuffs around his wrists. The coarse, rusty metal rubbed against his wounds, reopening them and sending blood to trickle down him like a river.

The shroud was removed, exposing his brutalized face. His beaten eyes were swollen nearly shut, and dark lines of exhaustion were chiseled in his cheeks. He tried to focus on his surroundings, but everything was a blur. As he hung there, he could make out walls and a floor of porcelain tiles. He looked up and realized there was no roof over his head. There was an apparatus above him, and the chain of the handcuffs was straddling a hook that was attached to it. In a moment, the apparatus emitted frigid water, engulfing his body. It felt as if it were biting into his skin. There was an opening in front of Erik which may have housed a door at one time. The room was filled with a mechanical hum, as if there were a presence lurking in the shadows. Erik sensed something there.

Erik perked up once he heard a voice. "Well, well. I bet you wish you were dead."

The creaking wheels of a cart echoed through the room as it slowly emerged from the shadows. Erik concentrated his attention on the toneless, guttural voice. "I told you that we would meet again." Erik stared into the deep abyss of Apophis's eyes as he spoke.

For the last five days, Apophis used torture and verbal intimidation methodically as tools to obtain the information he needed. All that time, he tried different ways to get Erik to tell him where the Anglo-Americans were going to land, trying to wrest it from him by layering different forms of agony on the general. To get what he wanted, he even tried to push Erik's buttons. Apophis had no time to waste since Himmler had pressured him. There was no doubt that Erik had out-thought Apophis's various verbal tricks to make him unintentionally reveal information. So, if psychological chicanery would not find cracks in the man's defenses, Apophis was left only with brute force.

Erik struggled to open his swollen eyes and focus on what was on the cart, barely making out a car battery with red and black clamps attached to it, with a set of sponges clamped at the other end of the long cables. The battery was also wired to a box with a nob on it.

Apophis stared at Erik with a callous, malicious smirk filled with venomous undertones. "I know," Apophis glanced at the battery, "you are wondering what this is for."

Erik took several deep breaths, knowing he had experienced no greater pain than what was coming and there was no way to prepare for it.

Apophis continued. "Some call this electroconvulsive therapy. I heard it was first developed in the late 1930s to treat patients with certain types of mental illness, including severe depression, severe mania, and catatonia." He stepped closer to Erik. "Want to hear something funny?"

"That you are a whacko psychopath and you get off on this?"

Apophis sighed and shook his head. "Oh, Erik, I would like you to know I call this *singing in the rain*. I daresay you'll be shocked by how well it makes you sing." He chuckled. "You are the tenor in this opera, and I'm simply here to provide motivation."

Erik's breaths came in rapid gasps as his heart threatened to beat through his ribs and leap from his chest.

"The car battery is an amazing invention. Do you know how much power this produces?" Apophis flashed an unnerving grin. "No?" He picked up the clamps holding the sponges and said, "Let's find out."

A wave of pain flooded Erik's body as Apophis touched the sponges to him. Every muscle tensed until they felt they were going to snap. His teeth ground together, and though he wanted nothing more than to scream, every muscle in his throat contracted so tight he could do nothing more than emit a barely audible groan.

Apophis pulled the cables away and waited a few moments before asking, "Where will the landings occur?"

Erik's eyes narrowed. "As you said, we are going to be here for a long time."

"Then we both have time to savor this experience."

Apophis touched the electrified sponges to Erik's chest. As current coursed through his body, it felt as if millions of scorching needles were shooting through him. He convulsed, and his veins swelled until it felt they were about to burst. When Apophis pulled the leads away again, after he regained control of his body, Erik let out a guttural scream.

"Tell me where the landings will occur," Apophis demanded. When he received no answer, he turned the knob on the machine and once gain held the sponges against Erik's body, that time for thirty seconds.

Erik's skin burned as his body whipped from side to side and back and forth. All he could hear was the buzzing of the current, his pulse exploding in his temples, and the cracking of teeth as he ground them together.

Apophis stopped and stared at Erik. "The landings?"

"I already told you. Pas de Calais."

Apophis shook his head. "I really don't believe you. I do believe in being thorough." Apophis turned the dial again, then ran the sponges slowly from Erik's upper chest to his stomach, then over his groin.

Erik felt like his joints were tearing apart as his muscles hardened and wrenched his body out of shape. His back arched until it felt like his spine would snap in half. After thirty seconds of pure hell, Apophis stopped. Exhausted, Erik hung with his teeth clenched and sucked in air through his nose. He stared at Apophis as urine dribbled down his leg.

Apophis turned to Erik as if he were an acquaintance at work rather than a man being tortured. He grinned as he spoke in a conversational tone. "Oh, yes. Here is something you might be interested in." He reached into his pocket and pulled out a folded piece of paper. As he unfolded it, he glanced at his watch.

Erik caught sight of the time. 1:50 in the morning. Erik had no idea what day it was, but he'd been there long enough that the sixth of June couldn't be far away. It could even be the sixth, for all he knew. Apophis would have to turn up the heat if he was running out of time. If that were the case, things could turn out very badly for Erik.

A smirk grew across Apophis's face as he said, "This is a communiqué from my people in London. 'To lead horticulturist.'" Apophis pointed to himself. "'Excavation team has the flower,' your wife." He gave a cunning grin. "'Will be delivered within two hours or less, depending on when the florist can make a delivery.'" With grace, he held the paper up.

Erik blinked through vision blurred by the electrical shocks and blows to his head but couldn't make out the writing.

Apophis looked at his watch again and tilted his head up with a venomous sneer. "My, my. It's nearly that time." Then, he pulled out the photograph of Jamie. "Erik, is she Jewish?"

Erik said nothing.

"Don't matter; I am going to enjoy taking my scalpel, cutting her from just below her breasts to her privates, and watching her bowels spill out." Apophis noticed the rage in Erik's eyes. "Or you can tell me where the landings will occur, and I will shoot her in the head, but only after I have my way with her in front of you." Apophis stared at Erik. "It's up to you."

There was a solid knock on the door shortly after that. Apophis remained stoic and acted as if that were what he was expecting.

As Apophis turned his back, Erik raised his knees to his waist. He took several deep breaths as his groin spasmed in pain. The door creaked open. He struggled against the handcuffs, but they held firm. However, he noticed they were simply draped over a hook. If he could get high enough he could free himself.

Giving up on breaking free in that moment, he focused on the conversation at the door, trying to figure out how dire his situation was. He also tried to locate a key to the handcuffs, perhaps on the table where the car battery was. Nothing. Could Apophis have the key?

The individual at the door addressed Apophis as Herr Colonel and clicked his heels. Erik surmised he was of a lower rank.

"I'm inches from breaking him," Apophis muttered. "Herr Sergeant, this had better be important."

The sergeant nodded and handed over a message.

"In ancient Greece, you would have been killed for this," Apophis stated as he began skimming the document.

The sergeant recoiled for a moment, then pressed on. "Sir, we heard from General Marcks's headquarters. They have reports of dummy paratroopers and landing in the Normandy area."

"Rubber dummies?"

"Yes, sir. In addition, there are reports that the Freya radar system site at Bruneval has picked up a large fleet was approaching Pas de Calais."

This is it, Erik thought. *It* is *the sixth, and the invasion has already started. Their radar was picking up chaff released to distract them from the real flotilla.*

Apophis dismissed the sergeant, slammed the door behind him, and walked toward the cart. He reached for the vial of Mescaline, grasped a syringe with his other hand, and drew out thirty ccs of the drug.

Erik took shallow breaths, peering down into Apophis's eyes with defiance.

"Why are there dummy paratroops landing in the Normandy area?"

Erik didn't respond.

Apophis grabbed the electrified sponges, and Erik tensed up. "Why are there dummy paratroops landing in the Normandy area?"

"A decoy," Erik mumbled.

Apophis slapped Erik and shouted, "Stop lying!"

"A decoy." Erik glanced down at the syringe. Was it morphine or something more sinister? *Either way*, he thought, *would be a relief. Maybe it'll end the pain or simply end me.* Then, Erik focused and remembered a day when he was in training at the farm.

You know what to do to survive.

You let moments pass and wait for the right opportunity.

You remember your training.

Day after day, you might never use what you learned.

But before you know it, without even realizing it, the paramilitary operative in you emerges.

Then, the training goes on autopilot, and all you have to do is survive.

Apophis stepped closer, and Erik raised his knees to his chest and kicked out, the balls of his feet striking Apophis's chest. The colonel dropped the syringe and stumbled across the room. Erik shimmied up the tile wall, lifted the chain off the hook, and landed on his feet. He then charged at the colonel.

Apophis pulled out his Luger and took aim, but Erik shifted his weight to the ball of one foot and raised his opposite knee, then kicked out, sending the luger flying across the room. As he pulled his leg back and stepped forward, Erik thrust his elbow into Apophis's jaw. Blood and teeth went flying, and the colonel spun around and stumbled across the room.

Erik's strength and energy were nearly drained. His muscles and joints swelled as pain rippled throughout his body. He stepped back, taking advantage of the opportunity to catch his breath. He remembered in training; they repeated a quote from G.I. Jane: "Pain is your friend. Your ally. It will tell you when you are seriously injured, it will keep you awake and angry, and remind you to finish the job and get the hell home. But you know the best thing about pain. It lets you know you're not dead yet!" The only thing that kept Erik going was instinct. Instinct to fight, to win, and finally, to kill.

Apophis tasted his own blood for the first time in his life. Trying to shake off the attack, he whipped his head up and shook it. His face tightened up in a mask of hate, his eyes filled with a blood-lust rage. He clenched his hand around his SS officer dagger, drew it, and grinned up at Erik. Like a hunter about to attack his prey, Apophis analyzed the situation.

Erik took several deep breaths and slowly exhaled as he focused on the blade and studied Apophis's hand and foot movements. The dagger was double-edged, which would make it harder to disarm the colonel. Harder, but not impossible. He looked up, met Apophis's eyes, and said through clenched teeth, "Since this will be your last night alive, I recommend you pay close attention. I will kill you. I will make you suffer unimaginable pain before I kill you. During your last moments, you will beg and pray for death."

Without further warning, Erik charged forward and kicked out at his foe's knee. Apophis sidestepped and thrust out with the knife, but Erik twisted aside and pushed Apophis's hand away. The colonel brought the dagger around and slashed Erik's forearm, then settled into a rhythm of weaving from side to side as he moved the knife in circles before himself, hoping to confuse Erik and get another slash in. The blade flicked out, thrusting toward Erik's abdomen over and over, causing the American to withdraw.

With a venomous tone and a dark, smoldering expression, Apophis said, "I'm surprised you can still fight."

"You put a lot of work into breaking me down," Erik smirked, and his eyes sharpened as they studied Apophis. "You failed."

Apophis moved his dagger from side to side in circular motions. He thrust the tip up toward the center of Erik's chest. Erik took a step back and batted the colonel's hand to the side. Apophis performed several horizontal thrusts from side to side without hesitating. Every time the dagger lashed out, Erik took a step back as he searched for a weapon.

His eyes landed on a pen on the cart. He feigned slipping and fell to his knees, his body twisted to expose his back. He reached for the cart, seemingly attempting to steady himself, and grabbed the pen. Apophis advanced to finish him, wrapping his left forearm around Erik's neck and bringing the dagger around for the kill. Erik smashed the ball of his palm against Apophis's elbow, pushing the blade away, then grabbed hold of his wrist and yanked it down.

The blood drained from Apophis's face, his eyes transfixed in horror, as his elbow popped, and his arm bent backward. Erik pulled harder and bones tore through flesh, jutting from Apophis's mangled arm in a spray of crimson. The dagger fell from the colonel's limp fingers, clanged on the tile floor, and skidded across the room. Erik struck again, driving his elbow into Apophis's crotch and sending the colonel stumbling back, gasping in pain. Erik rose to his feet, spun around with the pen in a white-knuckled grasp, and stabbed out at the Nazi's belly. He stabbed Apophis again, and again, and again, losing count after a dozen thrusts of the improvised weapon.

The colonel gasped, his eyes wide, more from surprise or pain, even he wasn't sure. As his life-giving blood flowed from his arm and belly like waterfalls, he collapsed to his knees. He paled as scarlet rivers flowed between the white tiles to unceremoniously gurgle past the steel drain in the center of the floor.

Erik stood over the colonel and tossed the pen onto the blood-soaked tiles. "Normandy," he said.

Apophis looked up with a dazed expression, not seeming to understand.

Erik tore the watch from the colonel's wrist. It was two in the morning. The airborne troops were already on the ground. "You wanted to know where the invasion would happen? Normandy, and we're already there."

Apophis started to laugh, then gagged and coughed, sending blood spewing from between his lips and dribbling down his chin. "I was right." He smiled as he looked up at Erik. "I was right the entire time."

"Yeah," Erik said, "but it's too late to do anything about it. You know what the most satisfying thing about this is going to be? It's that you're not the only Nazi that'll die this morning." Erik placed his hands on both sides of Apophis's face and drove his thumbs into the man's eyes. "I'll see you in hell." Apophis screamed as his eyes burst, then Erik twisted his head around until the sound of cracking bones echoed from the tile walls.

Erik pushed Apophis's lifeless body away. He then dropped to his knees and took the photograph of Jamie from the man's pocket. He also found the key for the handcuffs in another pocket and removed the restraints. Erik didn't know if D-Day would be successful, but he succeeded in his mission. The Germans would be in a state of panic and confusion, caught totally unprepared, as it was supposed to happen.

CHAPTER 27

TODAY IS HELL, BUT IT ENDS WELL

"That night I took time to thank God for seeing me through that day of days and prayed I would make it through D plus one. And if, somehow, I managed to get home again I promised God, and myself that I would find a quiet piece of land someplace and spend the rest of my life in peace."

— Richard D. Winters, *Band of Brothers*, "Day of Days"

HARDELOT CASTLE, CONDETTE, FRANCE, JUNE 6, 1944

The morning began as most mornings do, with Himmler sitting in an office at seven a.m., having his breakfast, sipping his coffee, and eating a piece of toast with marmalade as he read the daily press. The orderly brought in foreign press papers, reports of air raids that took place the night before, and any state matters that needed to be addressed by the Reichsführer as soon as possible. As soon as he finished, he left the office. Himmler immediately headed to the encryption team of Apophis's organization. While Himmler was traveling to the location, he pondered what the day was going to be like. Would it be a glorious day with the Allied armies defeated at the beaches? Could the allies have been attacking Pas de Calais at that time? Himmler nodded and continued on with his business. Soon after, he reached the encryption team. There was a question in his mind about whether there had been any new messages from the Royal Botanical Garden Society. The operator handed latest message over to him.

```
TO LEAD HORTICULTURIST: EXCAVATION TEAM HAS
NOT FOUND THE FLOWER.
```

By the crumbling up of the paper in his hand, the operator knew that Himmler had finished reading the message. Eventually, the alarm ceased to sound. It was only then that Himmler's attention was drawn back to the operator of the encryption team. "Herr Reichsführer," the operator started.

Himmler stared at the operator, as if to say, *What is it you want from me? Why are you bothering me?*

"Several of our headquarters confirmed throughout the night that some sort of widespread attack was in progress around the Normandy coast in the early hours of the morning."

Himmler tilted his head in disbelief.

"Early in the morning, off the coast of Normandy, around six am, our coastal defenses spotted Allied ships and planes deploying in astounding numbers. Both men and tanks were coming ashore."

Even though Himmler's temples throbbed with rage, he could still control himself as he allowed the significance of those words to sink in. One by one, with a short sideways jerk of his hand, he dismissed the subject. He scowled at the lieutenant and asked where Colonel Adelram was.

"I'm not sure, Herr Reichsführer."

Himmler instructed him to find him as soon as possible.

Suddenly, the lieutenant detached himself from the conversation and from Himmler's sight.

Within a few minutes, the lieutenant reported back with a certain amount of hesitation. "Herr Reichsführer, the last time we heard from Colonel Adelram, he was still interrogating the prisoner. That was approximately two-hundred hours."

Himmler glanced down at the dial of his wristwatch. It had been nearly five hours.

Himmler marched down the dank hallways toward the interrogation area, accompanied by the lieutenant and two soldiers with their fingers tense on their MP40 submachine guns' triggers. They stomped through the damp stone corridors, their footsteps echoing off the walls. Himmler ordered the soldiers to kick the door open as soon as they reached the room, and to secure it before he entered. Then, Himmler and the lieutenant stepped in.

Himmler's pulse throbbed in his temples as he stared down at the body of Apophis, mangled, bloody, and naked. The lieutenant ordered the soldiers to turn over Apophis's body. There was a hush in the room as they slipped across the wet, blood-soaked tiles, and everyone gasped as Apophis's eyeless visage was turned to look up at them. Himmler struggled to maintain his composure as he mumbled, "What the hell?" Himmler spun to face the lieutenant. "How in the hell did the prisoner walk out without being seen?"

"Herr Reichsführer, I don't know."

"Herr Lieutenant, are you telling me the man vanished like a ghost?"

"No, Herr Reichsführer!"

"I want him found! I don't care what you were doing prior! I want the prisoner found now!" He paused for a moment. Suddenly, the alarm rang, reverberating throughout the entire Château. Himmler looked up, wondering what was going on. A SS sergeant burst into the room and informed him that two guards were found dead, their necks broken, just outside the Château, and one outpost had not reported in. Eventually, the alarm was silenced.

Himmler's narrowed eyes focused on the lieutenant. "Find him now."

Not long after that, Himmler headed to the main conference room. The space was a scene of chaos, a cacophony of ringing phones, clacking Teletype machines, and rushing, confused analysts. Himmler glanced around, trying to locate a person of authority to find out what was happening.

"Herr Reichsführer." A senior officer approached Himmler. "Should we call the Führer and advise him of the situation in Normandy?"

"The invasion at Normandy is a decoy," Himmler said. "We don't need to wake the Führer for trivial things. The actual invasion will occur here at Pas de Calais, and we will be prepared for them. The Seventh Army will be able to hold off any attack the Allies put forth. I think you overestimate their chances of winning." He went back to hovering over the long map table and waited impatiently for reports on Normandy and Erik.

***

An SS captain marched across the parade grounds of the Château. SS soldiers scrambled to get in order. Standing at attention in military formation, their faces were rigid and stark, weapons poised and ready for orders. They all wore greenish-grey uniforms, each with distinct black collar taps to identify their rank on the left and the dreadful SS on the right, showing their affiliation with the infamous organization. As Opel Blitz trucks moved into place along the perimeter, the captain climbed into the back of a Kübelwagen and prepared to give his briefing. In the midst of the chaos, a lieutenant emerged, and the captain met him with cold eyes.

"Sir, the men are assembled and waiting for further orders."

"Have the men loaded into the trucks. We are trying to find a prisoner. This comes from the Reichsführer himself," he responded in a tone that could best be described as brusque, authoritative, and confident. The lieutenant and captain exchanged salutes.

As the lieutenant strode into the parade grounds, he barked an order to all the men in the area. Within a few minutes, the Kübelwagen and a half dozen Opel Blitz troop trucks were loaded with eighty soldiers. After a few moments, engines roared to life. One by one, they left, forming a column and turning left on Avenue Des Étangs. The SS captain was determined to find the missing prisoner—this *American* named Erik, according to his briefing—and believed he wouldn't come quietly.

He placed himself in the man's shoes. Getting into the prisoner's mind, he assumed Erik knew the SS soldiers would have the skills to track him down. The man would head to the beach and wait for the Allied armies to land. He figured Erik knew that whatever he did, it wouldn't be enough, because the Waffen SS would pursue him relentlessly.

At the corner of the avenues Des Étangs and Jean Garaialde, there was a guard post that was to check individuals who were trailing on the roads. The captain ordered his driver to halt and motioned to have some troops flank the area. After searching the guard post, a sergeant approached the Kübelwagen and reported. There were two dead. One was shot in the head while the other had a broken neck, just like the other guards.

"You and a few men will stay here. Radio headquarters and advise them of the situation. I will continue on to the beach." They exchanged salutes, and the pursuit resumed.

The captain looked back and gestured to the forward driver to follow as the column turned right on Avenue Jean Garaialde. The roar of the engines rumbled through the trees. The captain and driver kept alert for the French resistance as the road twisted and turned into Avenue des Bois. Because of the resistance, limited visibility, and poorly marked roads, the convoy remained in strict formation, with intervals of around thirty-five meters between each vehicle and speeds under forty kilometers per hour. It was almost too quiet, as if at any minute, they would be ambushed. The captain knew the beach was near because of the salty, briny breeze blowing through the air.

The column came to a halt at a checkpoint. The Kübelwagen was surrounded by MP40s pointed at the driver and the captain.

"Hold it right there!" a soldier barked at the driver.

"Papers!" another demanded of the captain with his gun pointed at him.

The captain pulled out his papers and handed them over.

The soldier called over his shoulder to his commanding officer, "It says here he is a captain from the Ausland-SD Amt VI[5] Section B[6], Herr Major."

The major approached the car and looked over the captain. Without looking at his subordinate, he stated, "He is." They exchanged salutes. "Herr Captain, are you here to give me an update on the allied invasion force?"

The captain shook his head. "I am looking for an escaped prisoner of war wearing an SS colonel's uniform. Did any of your men see him?"

The major shook his head as he replied, "No, Herr Captain." He pointed at the side of the road. "You can park there if you and your men want to commence a search on foot. My men need to be alert if the Allies land. Stay off the beach; it is mined."

The captain ordered the column to proceed. The tires of the vehicles ground over the dirt as they pulled off the road. The captain

---

5. Amt VI, "Foreign Intelligence Service

6. Section B was in charge of the Espionage in the West

climbed out of the Kübelwagen as the trucks behind him disgorged their eighty soldiers.

The sun slowly rose over the French coast as the wind blew, bringing a slight chill as dawn approached the coastline. Bunkers dotted the beach, accompanied by twenty millimeter anti-aircraft guns and several heavy artillery batteries, each protected by massive concrete blockhouses making up part of the Atlantic Wall.

Lookouts stared into the distance at the gray water of the English Channel with straight, foamy, white waves headed for the shore. The crews of the anti-aircraft and artillery batteries stood poised and ready to respond to any attacks headed their way.

The captain strode along the edge of the road overlooking the coast. He raised his binoculars and craned his neck to observe his surroundings. After focusing his eyes through the lenses, he scanned the horizon toward the beach and swept his gaze east and west toward the coastline. His eyes were captivated by the sight of four heavy guns within their own massive concrete emplacements.

The guns would prevent landing craft from reaching the shore and protect them from tanks. In the thrashing surf, the Allies would face a hellish environment. Getting ashore would entail passing over antitank ditches and crawling through minefields. Only then would they reach a fifteen-foot-high hedge of barbed wire, and beyond that were more minefields before the bunkers. A maze of machine-gun-filled trenches covered every inch of the headland behind the bunkers, and a garrison of two hundred armed men were ready to occupy them. Fortifications like that ran up and down the coast. The coastal defenses were impregnable and deadly.

Several members of the captain's detail combed along the rocky edge of the beach, trying to locate any sign of the prisoner. They searched the bunkers where he might be hiding. Men scoured through the brush and rocks along the slope.

Suddenly, the captain noticed that one of his men was signaling him to get his attention. The soldier called out, but at that distance, it was difficult for the captain to understand what the man was trying to say. Another soldier with a Feldfunk-Sprecher B two-way radiotelephone ran over to the man, and the soldier gave an update on the search.

"What did you find?" The captain demanded.

"A belt and a tunic of a colonel." The soldier fished the uniform out of the rocks. "The belt has a gun in the holster."

Just then, another soldier yelled and pointed to the beach near him. The captain lifted his binoculars and focused on where the soldier was pointing.

"What in the hell were you thinking?" He scanned a trail in the sand from the rocky coast to the edge of the shoreline, appearing as if someone had recently crawled through. "You'd have to be crazy to do that." He shook his head and realized he was looking in the wrong direction. He raised his binoculars and scanned further out, over the water. It never once occurred to him that someone would even attempt to do such a thing.

It was impossible for the SS captain to comprehend what Erik had gone through, death stalking him as he edged his way toward the channel. Perhaps he was too afraid to consider it. As he scanned the water, a floating object bobbed up and down in the binoculars' lenses. It was too far out to be sure, but the captain had a feeling it was a Luftwaffe rescue buoy. During the early stages of the Battle of Britain, they were designed to provide shelter for the pilots or crew of aircraft shot down over the sea. Even if Erik managed to reach the shore through the minefield, the captain couldn't fathom him reaching the buoy. The water was around fifteen degrees Celsius. Not only that, but the Channel was filled with jellyfish and other terrors of the deep. If he hadn't been stung and paralyzed by the jellyfish or eaten by a shark, surely the brazen American had succumbed to the frigid waters and drowned.

The captain lowered his binoculars and signaled for his men to call off the search. They would not find their escaped prisoner, as he'd already been swallowed by the sea.

***

As Erik stumbled down the rocky, moonlit beach, he thought the entire time, *I will struggle through. I will find a way to fucking survive.* He passed through razor-sharp, coiled barbed wire, several rows of hedgehogs[7] with mined tips, ramps[8], teller mines[9], and Belgium Gates[10]. He crawled as roaring waves lapped at the shore. The full moon blanketed the beach and the channel with a soft shimmer highlighting the crests of the waves and giving them a whitish-yellow glow.

His pulse thrumming in his neck, Erik cautiously crawled, and his terror mounted with every shimmy forward. Fighting through the fog of pain and exhaustion, he focused as the dagger penetrated the sand, listening and feeling for the telltale clunk of the blade striking the side of a mine. When he heard it, he was paralyzed by fear. He carefully navigated around the mine, adrenaline rushing through his veins as he pressed the dagger ahead, aware there

---

7. These were six-foot high steel obstacles designed to rip the bottom of landing crafts.

8. These were mine-tipped log obstacles designed to hit the bottom of landing crafts.

9. These were angled tip mine-tipped obstacles designed to hit the bottom of landing crafts. They were placed 200 yards from shore.

10. These were ten-foot-high steel wall obstacles, with anti-tank mines on top, placed parallel to the coast designed to hit the bottom of landing crafts.

could be another merely feet away. His hypersensitivity kicked into overdrive as he focused, making him more alert to his surroundings, but also bringing new waves of pain as gravel, salt, and sand ground into his wounds.

Each time he dragged himself forward toward freedom, nausea overwhelmed him. He crawled like that, probing a few inches ahead, then dragging himself a few inches along, for well over five hundred yards to reach freedom.

He fought back the chaos of his mind as sweat ran into his eyes as the bitter flavor of bile flowed into his mouth. He swallowed, the acid burning the back of his throat, and pressed on.

As Erik finally plunged into the cold water and began swimming, he focused on the mission. When others tried to change history to suit their purposes, he would be there to put things right. He was a man out of time, a man who did not exist, fighting for the betterment of humanity and restoring history to its proper course.

George Santayana once said, "Those who cannot remember the past are condemned to repeat it." Erik liked to joke, "Those who change the past are condemned to have a disastrous future."

He continued swimming, fighting off the cold and pain with every stroke. He fought to preserve an ideal that never should have existed in the first place: the preservation of history rent asunder by those who would meddle with the past.

What other historical events he knew of could be the result of a change somebody made? How many times had things been pushed toward a new end? He couldn't know for sure, but when he did find out somebody altered the timeline, he would volunteer to go back and set things right.

Erik's hand brushed against metal. He felt from side to side, finding a solid wall. He reached up and grabbed hold of a railing, then rubbed the water from his eyes. He hung from the side of what he recognized as a German rescue buoy, bobbing in the rough surf of the channel. He pulled himself around to the side, then laughed at the irony as he climbed up the ladder. Standing atop his new sanctuary, he looked to the northwest, toward England and safety.

Why am I always the one to volunteer to go back to the past? He asked himself as he climbed inside the buoy.

Because he was the best hope humanity had for the future.

ABOUT THE AUTHOR

Erik Foge holds a Bachelor's Degree in History, with an emphasis on Russian history and politics, from the University of Central Florida. His passion for history began at age thirteen when his parents sent him to Washington D.C. to learn about the United States and its governmental processes. The trip sparked Foge's interest in the federal government and the individuals within the Intelligence Community who are responsible for shaping the country's national policies. The characters in the *Project Pegasus Series* are drawn from his friendships and interactions with people from within the Intelligence Community at-large: the NRO; the NSA; the CIA; an Admiral and the Master Chief of the Sixth Fleet; Navy Seals, Astronaut John Glenn, and others.